Boyd isn't a great hunter, but he has principles, so when his leader asks him and the rest of the hunters to kill a child, he's out of there. Luckily for him, he and the others are welcomed by Rowan in his new clan, so they go from living in an abandoned warehouse to having their own houses.

But Boyd still isn't a great hunter.

When Alexis hears that someone is building a new Krsnik clan, he's curious but wary. He misses that sense of community, and his best friend is going whether he likes it or not, so they head there and pray the village will become a new home.

It does. Alexis meets his mate, and things are almost too good to be true.

Boyd doesn't want to continue hunting Kudlaks, even though that's why he's there, and worse, the Kudlaks are organizing, something they've never done before. Will Rowan kick Boyd out when Boyd tells him he's done with hunting? Is the village safe from the Kudlaks, or is this only the beginning of a new war?

Alexis
Copyright © 2023 Catherine Lievens
ISBN: 978-1-4874-4010-7
Cover art by Angela Waters

Published by eXtasy Books Inc

Look for us online at:
www.eXtasybooks.com

ALEXIS
KRSNIK CLAN 2

BY

CATHERINE LIEVENS

CHAPTER ONE

Boyd stuffed his clothes into his backpack. For once, he wasn't sorry that he owned so little. It came in handy now that he was running—now that Clay and Rowan had offered a way out.

"We're really doing this?" Kendrick asked from behind him.

Boyd turned toward him and gestured at him to pack faster. "We are, and if you don't want us to leave you behind, you're going to have to move."

"Being a hunter is all I know."

Boyd sighed. He doubted Clay would leave without them, but he wasn't sure about Clay's mate, Rowan. The two of them had come back after Rowan had kicked Cornelius's ass yesterday, just like they'd said. They'd offered to take the people who disliked how Cornelius did things with them. Boyd was one of those people, as were Kendrick and a few others.

Boyd had no idea what would come next for them, but he knew he couldn't stay one second longer. He'd hated following Cornelius's orders for a while, especially since Cornelius had become more bloodthirsty, and he finally had a way out. He wasn't going to give it up or mess things up.

Not too much, anyway. He had a knack for messing things up, though, so he wouldn't be surprised if Clay and his mate ended up giving him the boot.

He turned to look at Kendrick. "Don't you think it's the same for me? I've been a hunter for so long that I doubt I'd be able to do anything else. I don't want to continue following

Cornelius's orders, though. What he's been doing isn't right, and I refuse to go along with it. If that means I can't be a hunter anymore, then so be it. I won't hurt innocent people just because of what they are, especially children."

Kendrick still looked a little lost. Boyd wasn't sure what to say to make him see that this didn't have to be a bad thing. He hadn't spent a lot of time with Rowan, but he knew Clay fairly well, and Clay was a hunter through and through. He was a good hunter, too. He wouldn't give up the hunt just because he was leaving Cornelius and his group of hunters. Clay had never been part of their hunter family, but he'd shown everyone that it was possible to do this on his own.

Besides, Boyd wouldn't be on his own.

Boyd strode toward his friend and grabbed his shoulders. He gave Kendrick a little shake, and that seemed to do the trick.

"You don't have to stop being a hunter," Boyd said. "I don't know what's going to happen, but Clay and Rowan asked anyone who wanted to go with them to do so. That sounds like they're planning to create their own hunter group. That means you'll still be a hunter."

And so would Boyd. He wished he could be at least a little happy about that.

Kendrick finally nodded. "You're right. Besides, if I don't like the way they do things, I can still leave, right?"

"Yeah. Just like we're leaving now."

Boyd wanted to go as quickly as possible, but he couldn't deny that he was a bit anxious. Just like Kendrick, being a hunter was all Boyd knew. The life he had before was like a distant memory or maybe a dream. He remembered the reason he'd become a hunter, but even that felt distant. It was almost as if his sister had never existed, and he shook his head as he turned back to his packing.

His sister had existed, and she'd died. She was why he'd

become a hunter, and he told himself that leaving Cornelius didn't mean he had to stop his mission to get revenge for her.

Even though she wouldn't want him to do this. Even though she wouldn't like it.

Even though she would want him to be happy.

He finished stuffing his last t-shirt into his backpack and closed it. Thankfully, Kendrick had finally started packing, and he was almost ready. It only took him a few more seconds, and then he followed Boyd out the door.

Boyd would be glad to see the back of the warehouse. He had no idea where he and the others would end up, but it couldn't be worse in this place. Rowan and Clay had mentioned Whitedell yesterday, but everything was still up in the air.

The warehouse was dark, massive, and damp. It was filled with the hunters who followed Cornelius, and while there weren't that many of them, living with them made the place feel crowded.

There were no traces of Cornelius, but Clay and Rowan were waiting in the middle of the main room where Rowan had kicked Cornelius's ass yesterday. Some of the hunters had gathered on the other side of the room and were keeping an eye on them, as if they expected them to go nuts and start killing people. It was stupid. Boyd had managed not to kill any of those assholes the entire time he'd been here. Why would he start now that he finally had a way out?

Boyd kept an eye on the hunters who were staying with Cornelius as he moved closer to Clay and Rowan. Rachel was already there, her backpack hanging from her shoulder. Her expression was grim, but she nodded at Boyd when he reached the group. Kendrick was behind him, and he looked around.

Boyd didn't have to ask to know who he was looking for.

"He'll be right here," he tried to reassure Kendrick, patting his shoulder.

"Maybe one of us should have gone with him."

"He's packing. He's not going to stay behind, especially if we're not."

"I take it we're expecting at least one more person to join us?" Rowan asked.

Boyd was a bit intimidated. He'd been hunting Kudlaks for years, and of course, he'd heard about Krsniks. He knew they were the opposite of Kudlaks, even though they shared some characteristics, like being able to shift into animals and drinking blood. Initially, that was why he'd been wary of Rowan. He'd expected him to be like Kudlaks, but he wasn't. He was a good person, even though he drank blood.

The thought made Boyd shudder in horror, but he tried not to show it. He didn't know what would happen to him or any of the hunters, but Rowan and Clay were their new leaders. He didn't want to make them think badly of him before they even started whatever they were going to do.

The sound of rushing footsteps made all of them look up. Chris burst into the room, looking like he thought he was late. He was, but they wouldn't have left without him.

He hauled his backpack higher on his shoulder and made a beeline for them, ignoring everyone else, including Linda, the hunter he had something going on with. Boyd didn't think it was a relationship, but they'd been sleeping with each other for a while now.

"Sorry," he said. "I'm ready."

Rowan nodded at him. He turned to Clay, and his expression softened. That made Boyd feel weird, and he looked away because he didn't want to intrude on a private moment.

"Are we waiting for anyone else?" Rowan asked.

Clay looked around. He was probably counting the hunters who would follow him and Rowan, and Boyd did the same. There weren't many of them, but a dozen hunters were better than nothing. It was certainly better than staying back and obeying Cornelius's orders to kill children and people who hadn't done anything just because they were Kudlaks.

Boyd's mouth went dry at the thought of what Cornelius had asked. He'd really wanted to kill a little girl because she was a Kudlak. He'd been ready to hurt a child because of something she had no power over.

When had he become so evil? Boyd couldn't deny that sometimes, as hunters, they did questionable things. It went with the territory, but he'd always tried to follow a code of honor. Maybe he'd been the only one.

He looked around. No, he wasn't the only one. He was surrounded by hunters who didn't want to hurt kids. They wanted to do this the right way, which was why they were ready to follow Rowan and Clay.

"Chris," Linda said, stepping forward.

For a second, Chris looked like he was panicking. He managed to school his expression, and when he turned to Linda, he appeared cool and collected. Boyd wanted to hug him, but Chris needed to do this on his own.

"You're not coming?" he asked.

Linda hesitated, then shook her head. "I still believe in our mission."

"So do I."

"Why are you leaving, then?"

"Because it's the right thing to do. I'm not going to hurt people who never did anything to deserve it. I thought it was a given for everyone here, but clearly, I was wrong."

He turned to Rowan and Clay. "I'm ready whenever you are."

Boyd stood up straighter. He was ready, too.

Or at least, he hoped so.

Alexis eyed the Kudlak. When was he going to leave the damn bar? Alexis had better things to do than stalk this guy for the rest of the night.

That wasn't entirely true. The only thing he had to do was to go back to the apartment and Caroline and Jonas, but that was better than sitting on a hard stool, drinking warm beer, and waiting for a Kudlak to choose his prey.

Alexis sighed and took another sip of his beer. He had to work hard not to grimace at the warm liquid, but he didn't want the Kudlak to realize he was here to stop him. If the Kudlak had been any good, he would have noticed him a while ago. Maybe if he had, Alexis would already be home.

But he wasn't.

He resisted the urge to pout and continued staring at the Kudlak. This was a supernatural bar, which meant that most people here didn't care what the Kudlak was. They wouldn't kick him out if he didn't attack anyone.

The Kudlak was dangerous, but then so was Alexis, as well as many people in the bar tonight. They could turn into animals or had fangs or other powers that meant they could hurt someone if they wanted to. Usually Alexis didn't, but Kudlaks were different.

They were evil and always had been. Alexis wouldn't say they were born that way, but most were raised to hunt and kill Krsniks and anyone else they wanted. They didn't care for human life. They only cared about themselves, and that made them dangerous.

"I don't know. I heard he contacted the council."

The conversation between two men a few stools down from the one Alexis was sitting on caught his attention. He never looked away from the Kudlak, but he needed something to distract himself from how boring this was. He wished he could go up to the Kudlak and drag him into the parking lot, but he was pretty sure the bouncers would kick his ass if he tried. As long as they were inside and the Kudlak didn't do anything he shouldn't, Alexis couldn't touch him.

"What's the council going to do? Give him what he wants?"

Alexis peeked at the two men talking. From the smell, one of them was some kind of feline shifter. He wasn't sure about the other one and didn't care.

The cat shifter rolled his eyes. "The council is going to give him what he wants. Isn't that what they always do? They give stuff away to the people they want."

"I wouldn't say it's for free. You know what Krsniks do." The man peeked at the Kudlak, who was focused on his phone.

The fact that these two guys knew what Krsniks and Kudlaks were got Alexis's attention. He didn't think they'd realized that he was a Krsnik, but they'd clocked the Kudlak as a Kudlak.

"That guy hasn't done anything dangerous since he arrived," the cat shifter said with a snort. "I don't think we need Krsniks to defend us from him or from any other Kudlak. I'm a lion shifter. If one of them tries to attack me, I'll kick their ass."

Alexis almost snorted. Of course the guy was a lion shifter. They tended to believe that they were stronger than anyone and could take on any attacker, but that was far from the truth. The lion didn't realize how dangerous Kudlaks could be. His friend seemed more careful, which was a good thing.

"Yeah, maybe," the other guy said, peeking at the Kudlak again. "But I'm still happy there are more Krsniks around. You know the Kudlaks have started organizing."

"So are the Krsniks if they're moving to this fucking village in Whitedell."

Alexis blinked. A village in Whitedell? What was the lion talking about? All Krsnik clans were gone. Kudlaks had decimated entire families, while others had perished in the wars. They didn't live in villages anymore. There weren't enough of them to do so. They lived alone or in small groups, like in Alexis's case.

He, Caroline, and Jonas hadn't belonged to the same clans. In a way, that should have made them enemies, but they'd never been. They'd been friends and family for as long as they'd known each other. They protected each other, and their last names had never mattered.

"We don't know that they're going there," the second guy said. "It's just a rumor."

"Not a rumor. My cousin's girlfriend works for one of the council members. She knows everything that's going on, and she told him that the council approved the use of a small, abandoned village for this new clan. Instead of putting a pride or even a pack there, they're giving the place to those freaks."

Alexis wanted to hear more, but the Kudlak got to his feet. His gaze was locked on a woman leaving the bar, and Alexis knew what he was planning. The Kudlak had been hunting, just like Alexis. They'd just been hunting a different prey.

Even though Alexis wanted to stay back and demand more details from the two guys talking, he followed the Kudlak outside. He wasn't surprised when the Kudlak went straight for the parking lot. In the distance, Alexis could see the woman who'd left the bar ahead of them stopping by a car. The Kudlak rushed ahead, but Alexis was faster.

He grabbed the Kudlak's shoulder, pulled him back, and used the element of surprise to stab the asshole in the heart.

The Kudlak's expression would have been comical if the situation hadn't been what it was. His eyes widened, and he looked down at his chest as if he couldn't believe Alexis had killed him. Alexis pushed him to the ground, then looked around to make sure no one had noticed anything.

The woman had gotten into her car and was leaving the

parking lot. Alexis waited until her car disappeared to take his knife back, clean it on the Kudlak's jacket, and rush over to his own vehicle. Now that the Kudlak had been taken care of, he could go home and tell Jonas and Caroline what he'd heard.

He didn't know what to think of the fact that someone was building a new clan. The Krsniks needed it. They'd been strong when they lived in clans and had big families. They'd killed many Kudlaks and saved many people who would have died otherwise. After the war, there were only a few of them left. They had to work on their own or in small groups, and it wasn't always easy or possible.

Alexis supposed he could stop being a hunter, but it was what he was born to do. It was his duty and mission to get rid of as many Kudlaks as possible, and the fact that he was doing so alone wouldn't stop him.

But it looked like he might not have to do it on his own. Maybe this new clan would welcome him and his friends.

Or maybe they'd kick them to the curb.

Alexis couldn't know what would happen, but he did know how Jonas would react to the news. That was why he didn't waste time telling him and Caroline as soon as he reached the apartment they shared.

"There's a rumor that someone's putting together a new Krsnik clan," he declared as he walked in through the door.

The two of them were on the couch, although Jonas was the only one wearing pajamas. Caroline had gone out hunting and was still wearing her hunting gear, but she'd removed her boots.

Both of them looked up, and Jonas's eyes went wide.

"A clan?"

Alexis nodded as he took off his jacket. "I don't know much, but I'll tell you everything I heard." And that included the fact that the new clan was located in Whitedell.

Whitedell was famous because one of the council members lived there, but that was all Alexis knew about it. He had no idea where the clan was located, who was in charge of it, or how many people they had. He also didn't know how they would react if he and his friends decided to go there. Having three Krsniks pop up on their doorstep might not get a good reaction out of them.

Alexis would deal with it once they got there. For now, he sat down on the floor by the coffee table and told his best friends that, just maybe, they weren't alone anymore.

Boyd was still nervous by the time they reached the motel. He'd expected Cornelius to try to stop them from leaving, but he hadn't seen the man since Rowan had kicked his ass. Cornelius hadn't tried to stop anyone, not even the people he considered his hunters. It seemed he'd given up on them, which Boyd felt was a good thing. It would have been a mess if Cornelius had ordered the other hunters to stop those who were leaving with Rowan and Clay. He hadn't, and now, they were free.

Boyd hadn't expected to feel so good about it, but he did. It was as if a huge weight had lifted from his shoulders, and he hadn't even known that weight was there.

"All right, everyone," Clay said, clapping his hands to get their attention. "We'll spend a few hours here. Rowan contacted the council, and we've been given our own village. We'll get some Nix to shimmer us there, but I feel like everyone needs some rest first. There's going to be a lot of work to do when we get there."

Boyd hadn't expected that. "What do you mean, a village?" he asked.

"Krsniks live in clans," Rowan explained quietly. "Or at least, we used to. Most of our clan was made up of family

10

members, but not only. We had Krsniks from other clans, as well as other supernatural creatures who lived with us. We used to live in big houses like some prides and packs do, but most of the time, we lived in villages. It gave everyone their own space."

He'd explained some of this yesterday, but Boyd had many more questions he didn't think he'd get the opportunity to ask today, and that was all right. There was only one question that felt important right now.

"And you have a village?"

Rowan and Clay had mentioned Whitedell, but Boyd hadn't been sure this was actually going to happen. It sounded too good to be true.

Maybe it wasn't.

"We do now. I called Dominic, the council member. He'd already told me that the council was interested in creating a village for a clan of Krsniks. They have proof that the Kudlaks are organizing and becoming more dangerous, and Krsniks are born to fight Kudlaks. That's why everything is going so quickly. The council expected me to contact them, and they knew what I'd need when I did."

"Where are we getting the money for all of this?" Kendrick asked.

Rowan sighed. He was probably tired and wanted some time alone with his mate, but Boyd felt they deserved at least some answers. He'd be the first to dive into the closest bed as soon as they had them.

"Dominic said that the council would fund us. We're not enforcers, but we'll be doing something similar, and we'll be paid for it. I already told you that I don't know how to lead a clan, and that hasn't changed, but I'll do my best. Now, get some rest and be ready to leave in a few hours."

Now that Boyd knew where they were going and how they were going to make this work, he felt better and ready to sleep forever. He only had a few hours, so he needed to be quick.

He eyed the Kudlaks. They were sticking close to Rowan and Clay, especially the young boy. Boyd knew he was human, but seeing the three of them together, they looked like a family. He felt a bit uneasy at having an adult Kudlak hanging around, but if Clay and Rowan trusted her, Boyd wasn't going to go against them. They were clan leaders, while he was just a hunter.

And one who didn't even like what he did.

He shook his head and grabbed one of the room keys from Clay. He and Kendrick were sharing a room, and neither of them spoke as they landed on the beds. Boyd couldn't remember the last time he'd slept in a bed with clean sheets and a door that closed.

"I don't know if anyone will be able to wake me up in a few hours," Kendrick mumbled.

"I'll slap you if you don't wake up," Boyd promised.

Then, for the first time in as long as he could remember, he closed his eyes and slept without being afraid of what would happen to him when he did.

Boyd had no idea what time it was when a knock on the door woke him up. He blinked his eyes open and looked out the window. It was still dark.

Kendrick was snoring in the bed next to Boyd's. He hadn't heard the knock, so Boyd got to his feet and went to open the door.

"We're ready to go," Clay said.

Boyd nodded. "Give me five minutes to wake up Kendrick, and we'll be there."

Clay nodded, then hesitated. "I'm glad you decided to follow us."

Boyd shrugged. "I wasn't going to stay back and kill kids. You know how bad I am at this, though, right? I don't know what kind of hunter I can be, but I promise I'll do my best."

"I have no doubt about that. Maybe we can talk later."

That didn't sound good, but Boyd nodded anyway. He wasn't going to say no to his clan leader.

It took him a while to wake up Kendrick, but once he did, they got out of the room in just a few minutes. Kendrick was still rubbing his eyes as they joined the others in the parking lot.

"I thought the Nix would already be here," he complained. "I could have slept for a few more minutes."

"But then you would have missed my grand entrance," a voice said.

A Nix with pink hair had appeared in the middle of their group. He opened his arms wide as if making sure everyone could see him.

It would have been hard to miss him. It wasn't only the pink hair. He was full of tattoos and piercings, but even more so, he was the most gorgeous man Boyd had ever seen.

"It's good to see you again," Clay said as he moved closer to the Nix.

He held out his hand to shake the Nix's hand, but instead, the pink-haired guy pulled him into his arms, making him squeak in surprise. Boyd bit his lower lip so he wouldn't start laughing.

"We're cousins," the Nix declared. "None of that weird handshake thing."

Once he was done hugging Clay, he turned to Rowan, who looked like he might make a run for it. The Nix caught him, and Rowan yielded, a resigned expression on his face as he hugged him.

Once he finished, the Nix turned to everyone else standing around them. For a second, Boyd wondered if he was going to hug all of them, but thankfully, another Nix appeared next to him. This one had long hair and no tattoos or piercings.

"What are you doing?" he asked. "We're just here to shimmer them to the village."

"I was making friends," the pink-haired Nix said.

The other one rolled his eyes and turned to their group. "My name is Ani. I'm the Whitedell pride's alpha mate. This is Nysys, one of our pride members. We're here to take you to your village. I'm sorry we couldn't take you there immediately, but Dominic insisted on sending someone to ensure everything was safe. Several houses need work, but you should all be able to find a place to settle down, and of course, the pride will help any way we can."

"Thank you," Clay said as he moved closer to the alpha mate. "You're doing a lot."

"The council is. They're really excited about having you guys on board."

That was good. If the council needed them, it meant they wouldn't try to arrest them. They were giving them a place to call home, and Boyd couldn't wait to see it.

So when Nysys held out his hands, Boyd was one of the first to grab him.

"This is going to be great," the Nix said with a wide smile. "I'm already organizing a party for this weekend."

Ani groaned, but if he said something to Nysys, Boyd didn't catch it, because Nysys had already shimmered them away.

"We need to go to that village," Jonas declared as he got to his feet.

Alexis was pretty sure he was ready to start packing. He'd expected this kind of reaction from Jonas, but that didn't mean they shouldn't be careful. They needed to be sure of what they were walking into, but if it was up to Jonas, they wouldn't even pause to check.

"We don't know if they'll want us," Caroline cautioned. "Actually, we don't know anything about this. We just have what Alexis heard."

"Isn't it enough? They're building a Krsnik clan. Don't you miss having a clan? Having people around you who can help and protect you?"

Alexis suddenly felt guilty. "Don't I protect you enough?"

Jonas rolled his eyes. "If anything, you're overprotective. That's not what I'm talking about, and you know it. I love the two of you, but I want more. I want people around me and to find my mate one day. I want a family and a place to call home." He gestured at the apartment. "This isn't home."

The apartment was decent, but Alexis understood what Jonas was talking about. The three of them had grown up in villages with their clans surrounding them, and Alexis missed it as much as Jonas did. He wanted to go back to that and feel like he had a family who would be there for him if he needed anything.

But they had to be cautious, because, like Caroline pointed out, they knew nothing about this new clan.

"They could be enemies of our old clans," Caroline said.

Jonas put his hands on his hips. "And even if they are? We're past that. The wars are over, and I don't care who these people are. They're trying to rebuild our race."

"By setting up a village?"

Alexis was skeptical, too, even though he wanted to believe in this. He couldn't afford to do that before he knew what was happening. He didn't want to hope only to be kicked in the teeth by whoever these people were.

"We don't know who they are or who they're including in their clan," he told Jonas. "We don't know anything about them except that this village is in Whitedell."

"Then that's where I'll be going." Jonas looked from Alexis to Caroline. "You know I love the two of you. You're my family, and I don't want to be away from you. I want this future, though. I need to give this a try, and if it doesn't work out, we can come back or move somewhere else. But I truly feel that this will be the best thing we can do for the future."

There was a war inside Alexis's mind. One side of him wanted to go along with Jonas and follow him to Whitedell without thinking too much about the consequences. Did it really matter when they might be about to find a new clan?

But the other part of Alexis was telling him to be careful. He only knew about the clan because he'd overheard a conversation between two shifters. What if they'd been lying?

He didn't see why they should have been. They were having a conversation between friends, and they hadn't noticed that Alexis was listening. He suspected that everything they'd said was true, or at least, that they thought it was. The lion's cousin's girlfriend might have heard things wrong, but even if she had, Jonas was not stopping. He'd be going to Whitedell, no matter what.

Caroline and Alexis would have to decide whether to follow him or stay back. Alexis didn't have to think about it. If Jonas was going, so was he.

He and Caroline looked at each other. She rolled her eyes, but she was smiling.

"Fine," Alexis said. "We'll go."

Jonas bounced on his feet and clapped his hands. "I knew you wanted it as much as I do."

"You're right. I want a clan, a village, and a place to call home. We need to be careful, though. We don't know anything about this village. We're not even sure who's in charge and what clan they belonged to. They could kick us out as soon as we get there or maybe attack us."

"I hate when you're so negative about everything," Jonas complained.

"I call it being realistic. I want to believe in this as much as you do, but my main goal is to protect the two of you. If the clan is dangerous, I'm grabbing both of you and running."

"Why would the clan be dangerous? They're Krsniks, like us. They're building a new clan, probably because they've been forced to hunt and live on their own like we have. We belong to the same race, Alexis. They have to want a home and a clan as much as we do."

Alexis and Caroline looked at each other again. Jonas might be right about that, but it still didn't mean the clan would welcome the three of them.

"We'll go there and see what happens," Caroline interjected. "If we see it's not for us, or anything is weird, we're coming back."

Jonas pouted. "Do we have to come back? I don't like this place."

Alexis didn't like their apartment in the middle of Oklahoma, either. "We'll go wherever you want."

That was enough to bring the smile back to Jonas's face. "Great. I'm going to pack, and you should do the same. I want to reach Whitedell by tomorrow." He paused and looked at Alexis. "We could use a Nix app."

Alexis was already shaking his head. "I want to take the truck. It'll be easier to carry our stuff, and that way we can get out of there quickly if they don't want us."

"Try to see the glass half full instead of half empty for once, Alexis. This is going to be great. We're going to have a clan again, and you and Caroline can continue hunting bad Kudlaks. I won't have to worry about either of you getting hurt anymore because I'll know you'll have backup."

This had never been easy for Jonas. He might be a Krsnik and had been born to hunt Kudlaks, but he'd never been a fighter, and he freaked out whenever he hurt someone. He wasn't a great hunter, but he didn't need to be. He was still family to Alexis and Caroline, and they both had a fierce need to protect Jonas and his innocence.

Having a clan would help. Not all Krsniks were hunters, just like not all hunters were Krsniks. If they found a place to call home in Whitedell, Jonas could finally do whatever he wanted with his life. So far, he'd worked in coffee shops and fast-food places because it was the easiest way for him to make money. It wasn't what he wanted, though, and he wasn't happy.

But maybe that was about to change. Alexis was afraid to hope, but as he watched Jonas walk away to start packing his stuff, he felt they were doing the right thing. Even if they found out they weren't welcome with the new clan, they needed out of this place.

"I'm worried," Caroline murmured.

Alexis tried to school his expression so she wouldn't see that he was, too. "Maybe Jonas is right, and we should look at the situation with optimism. It's the first time we've heard about a new clan being created since the clans disappeared. Whoever the leader is, they won't have enough Krsnik from their old clan to make up a new one. That means they'll need more people."

"Still doesn't mean we'll be welcome."

"Maybe not, but the three of us are a package deal. If any of us isn't welcome, we'll leave. Hell, we could even start a clan of our own."

Caroline snorted. "Sure we can. Who's going to be the leader? You?"

Alexis couldn't think of anything worse than having to lead an entire clan of Krsniks and other supernatural creatures. "I was thinking about you, actually."

"Not even if you paid me." She sighed. "We should start packing. You know Jonas is going to want to leave as soon as he's done."

He would, and like always, Caroline and Alexis would

give him what he wanted.

Hopefully they'd be able to. Jonas wanted nothing more than a clan and a place to call home.

And he wasn't the only one.

Chapter Two

When Boyd looked around, he still couldn't believe what he saw. How had he gone from living in an abandoned, cold warehouse with a bunch of people he disliked to having a home and living on his own?

Some would say he'd made the right choice when he'd decided to follow Clay and Rowan. He wasn't entirely sure he had yet, but he wanted to hope. So far, they hadn't asked anything he wasn't willing to give. They hadn't demanded he hurt someone or even go on a hunt. He'd seen surprisingly little of them as they settled in their new village, and while he didn't mind, he also wanted to get to know them better. They were his new leaders, after all.

Boyd relaxed on his couch and looked at the ceiling. He had a couch now. He also had a bed with a mattress and soft sheets, which meant he didn't have to sleep on the floor anymore. His back didn't hurt, and he actually felt rested when he woke up in the morning.

He'd known Clay for a few years now, but not well. Rowan, on the other hand, was a mystery. Boyd knew very little about him beyond the fact that he was a Krsnik and Clay's mate. He had many questions, but he suspected he wasn't the only one. Hopefully, Rowan would find a way to answer them without having to meet with every member of their new clan one by one. Boyd could only imagine how annoying that would be.

For now, everyone was too busy. After leaving the motel where they'd spent a few hours to rest the other day, they'd been shimmered to the middle of this village. The alpha mate of the Whitedell pride had assured them that they'd be able to shield the village so that no one could shimmer in except in the designated spots, but for now, it was a free for all, and Nysys was using that freedom liberally. He always popped up when people least expected him to, and he'd already made Boyd jump a few times.

When they'd arrived at the village, Boyd had expected him and the other hunters to be set up together in one of the houses. The village was nice, but it was clear that it had been abandoned a while ago and that no one had taken care of it. Most of the houses were still sturdy, albeit dusty, but some needed a lot of work. Thankfully, Kendrick had worked constructions before becoming a hunter, and he'd been ordering them around as they cleaned up and attempted to fix what they could. The Whitedell pride alpha had promised to send more people, which was good because some of the houses wouldn't be accessible until they made sure they weren't dangerous and fixed what needed to be fixed.

But most of the houses had been fine, and everyone had been assigned one. They'd even been able to choose which one they preferred, which wasn't something Boyd was used to. Even before becoming a hunter, he'd lived in rented apartments. Now, he had a massive house — or at least, what felt like a massive house to him. It had two stories, with three bedrooms and two bathrooms upstairs, which was way more than he needed. When he'd pointed that out, Clay had clasped his shoulder and told him to think of the future. Since Boyd was a clan member now, it meant he'd live here for the rest of his life. If he ever wanted a family, he'd need those empty rooms.

Boyd couldn't imagine having a family. He'd always believed he'd die being a hunter, and he'd come close a few times. He wasn't sure he'd want to continue hunting Kudlaks if he had someone waiting for him at home. The thought of abandoning them freaked him out, even though they weren't real.

Boyd's phone vibrated in his pocket. He slid it out and realized it was the alarm he'd set up earlier. It was still early in the morning, but the hunters had been training since they'd arrived, and today wouldn't be any different. The morning was dedicated to training and making sure they could face a Kudlak and survive, while the afternoons were spent fixing their homes and the village. There were houses, but also other buildings. The village had been mostly self-sufficient, which meant there was a small bakery, a grocery store, and a few other businesses that needed to be cleaned up, too. Boyd hadn't realized what Rowan meant when he'd explained they'd live in a village. He'd thought it would only be hunters, but that couldn't be further from the truth. For now, the majority of them were hunters, but that wouldn't be forever.

He pushed up from the couch and stretched. He got ready to leave and headed out. The air was cool, but it wasn't raining, which was a good thing. He wanted to check his roof later today, so he hoped the weather would hold.

For now, they were training in the space in front of the house Rowan and Clay had chosen for themselves. Rowan had promised they were thinking about an enclosed space they could use when the weather was bad, but everything that was big enough and available needed to be checked by someone who knew what they were doing when it came to buildings. The last thing they needed was for the roof to fall on their heads while they were beating each other up.

Boyd couldn't say he was looking forward to training. He especially wasn't looking forward to it when Rowan put him and Rachel together. Rachel grinned at him and wiggled her fingers while Boyd had to resist the urge to groan. Still, he wasn't going to say no to his leader's order, so he went.

And got his ass kicked.

That wasn't new, but it still hurt, not only physically.

"Are you okay?" Rachel asked as she came to stand over him.

This time, Boyd did groan. "Can you take it easy on me?"

"I might have to. What's going on with you?" She crouched next to Boyd and offered him her hand. "You've been distracted lately."

Boyd allowed her to pull him into a sitting position. "Don't you think there's enough to be distracted about?"

"Yeah, but not that badly. What if I'd been a Kudlak?"

She was right. If she'd been a Kudlak, Boyd would be dead, which was something he wanted to avoid. He couldn't help that he was distracted, though. He'd felt this way even before all of this happened, and while a lot had changed in his life lately, not everything had.

He still hated being a hunter.

He wasn't about to say that out loud. He got to his feet and brushed his hands on his pants, then looked around, hoping that would be enough for him today. Clay was staring at him, though, and Boyd needed to make sure no one realized just how much he hated being a hunter. He couldn't afford to be kicked out of the village for not pulling his weight. Besides, he did know how to fight. He just wasn't very good at it.

After he got his ass kicked by Rachel a second time, he decided to take a break. He could feel people watching him, and he disliked it intensely. It made him want to run, but he couldn't afford to. Instead, he grabbed a bottle of water and went to lean against the side of one of the houses.

That was where Clay found him. "Everything okay?"

Boyd quickly nodded. "Of course."

"Are you sure? Because I've been watching you, and I can tell your heart isn't in it."

Boyd quickly straightened. "What are you trying to say?"

His heart raced with the fear that Clay had realized that he didn't want to do this and was about to kick him out.

Clay raised his hands. "Just that if you don't want to be a hunter anymore, that's fine. No one is going to force you to do something you don't want."

"Of course I want to be a hunter. I haven't changed my mind about it, including killing as many Kudlaks as possible. They took my sister. I'm going to take everything I can from them."

Clay didn't look convinced. "I understand wanting revenge, but if it's the only reason you're doing this, maybe it's better if you take a step back."

Boyd snorted. "Revenge is the only reason most of us are doing this. I'm fine." Boyd really wasn't, but he couldn't afford to lose this. He might not want to be a hunter, but he wanted to be alone and homeless even less. If staying at the village and being a hunter meant he had a home and a place where he belonged, then he'd kill as many Kudlaks as he could to show Clay that he deserved a place here.

Alexis parked the truck and looked at the small village in front of them. "I thought they would have at least shielded this place," he grumbled. There were no guards or anything to protect the village and its inhabitants.

Jonas bounced in the backseat. "If they've only just arrived, they wouldn't have had time to set up protections. Besides, we haven't heard about any Vila living here. If there are only hunters, they don't have the magic to do anything."

He was right, but it didn't sit right with Alexis. If this place was going to be a Krsnik village, it needed to be safe. The way it was now, anyone could walk in and attack, including Kudlaks.

He told himself not to judge the village and their leader just yet. Jonas was right. These people had only just gotten here and needed time to prepare everything for the fight.

He and Caroline, who was in the passenger seat, exchanged a glance. She shrugged, and Alexis told himself to let it go. It wasn't like anyone would listen to him, anyway. Jonas was so excited that it was a miracle that he hadn't yet hopped out of the truck.

He proceeded to do just that a few seconds later.

Alexis swore and quickly opened his door. He scrambled out of his seat, rushing toward Jonas, who was striding toward the village.

"You don't know what kind of protection they have," he called out. "Don't be an idiot—come back here."

Jonas flipped him the bird, but thankfully he slowed down, then stopped.

For a moment, Alexis thought that Jonas had listened to him for the first time ever. Then he saw the man standing behind one of the houses.

The man was staring at them, which meant he'd seen them. There was no going back, even though Alexis wanted nothing more than to grab Caroline and Jonas and drag them back to the truck.

"Well, I'd say they know we're here," Caroline drawled.

"You're not helping."

She winked at him. She looked like she didn't have a care in the world today. Her long blond hair was loose around her face, and she wore makeup. Alexis couldn't remember the last time he'd seen her wearing makeup. She also wore her hunting gear, which meant she was dressed all in black. It was a sight to behold, even when she was relaxed.

A movement in Jonas's direction caught Alexis's attention. The man who'd been standing by the house was coming toward him, and he was still alone. Alexis didn't know if he was stupid or convinced he could defend himself against the three of them. He was about to find out either way.

The man stopped before reaching Jonas. Alexis quickly joined his best friend, and with Caroline on his other side, they faced the Krsnik in front of them.

Alexis had no doubt the guy was a Krsnik. He even knew what family the Krsnik belonged to. The violet eyes were a dead giveaway.

He inclined his head. "You're a Harper." Once, they'd been one of the biggest and most respected clans in the Krsnik world. He'd thought all of them had died, but he'd been wrong.

"I'm Rowan," the man said. "You're Krsniks."

"We are. I'm Alexis, and this is Jonas and Caroline."

Rowan cocked his head. "You heard about the village."

"Alexis did," Jonas interjected. He was so excited it was a miracle he wasn't bouncing around.

"And you decided to visit?"

Alexis cleared his throat before Jonas could explain what they were doing here. "We decided to come and see what was happening. There haven't been any clans since the wars."

Rowan nodded. "I'm very much aware of that. There is one now, though."

"I'm not saying we want to be part of the clan yet, but it's one of the reasons we're here." Alexis hesitated. He didn't want to spill his life history and didn't think he needed to. Rowan obviously knew what he'd gone through. He'd gone through the same thing. "We wanted to see if being part of this clan was a possibility."

"I really hope it is, because I'm not going back to Oklahoma," Jonas added.

That made Rowan smile. Alexis allowed himself to relax, but he kept an eye on Rowan. He didn't trust him yet, mostly because he didn't know him. The Harper clan had been respected because they were good people, but there was no way to know if Rowan had followed in his family's footsteps. So far, Alexis hadn't seen anything that would tell him he shouldn't trust the guy, but they'd just met. Given time, he was sure he could find something.

"Why don't you let me explain what happened and why we're building a clan?" Rowan asked. He gestured at the village. "You can even see the place if you want. There aren't many of us yet, but we're under the protection of the Whitedell pride. They only live about ten minutes away."

The warning was right there. If Alexis and his friends tried anything, they'd have to face the wrath of the Whitedell pride and the council.

Alexis didn't know where Rowan had come from, but he had powerful protectors.

He listened as Rowan guided them toward the village. He wasn't surprised to learn that Rowan had been on his own until recently. He hadn't even been working as a hunter. Alexis had nothing against that. Jonas never worked as a hunter, and even Alexis and Caroline sometimes had to take breaks. Hunting on their own or even together was dangerous because there were only two of them. Rowan was hunting again, though, and he was doing so with his mate. Apparently, the man was human, but he'd killed many Kudlaks and wasn't showing signs of slowing down. The couple was what every Krsnik leader should be like.

"So do you only take in Harpers?" Jonas asked. "Because we're not. Does it mean we can't be part of your clan?"

"Well, there's only one other Harper left," Rowan said. His expression turned sad. "My cousin is part of the Whitedell pride, so he won't be becoming part of the clan. He's not hunting anymore and has no intention of returning to it. He has children and a mate, and he's happy. All of this to say that it would be a tiny clan of one if I only took in people from my old clan."

"I feel that this is true for many other clans," Alexis murmured.

He was sure other members of his clan were still alive, but he'd never been able to find them. After the wars, they'd scattered, and they were still living all over the country and possibly out of it. It was sad, but his clan had been large, and he hadn't known most of the members well. He didn't miss them, but he did miss the sense of family that being with a clan brought.

"Clay and I are looking for anyone who wants to become a part of our clan," Rowan explained as they reached the center of the village.

It was like Alexis had expected. The place had seen better days, but it appeared solid and could become a home for many people. He could see himself living here, even though he hadn't made a decision yet.

He liked the place and Rowan, or at least what little he knew about him. He wasn't keen on returning to Oklahoma, either, and he could see himself, Jonas, and Caroline settling down here. It would be an adjustment, but maybe they'd finally found a place to call home.

"And having more Krsniks in our clan would be good," Rowan continued. "So far, it's only me, my mate, a bunch of human hunters, and a small Kudlak family."

Caroline stiffened. "Kudlaks?"

Rowan's expression hardened. "They're a mother, her child, and the human teenager she adopted. She's not dangerous and won't become dangerous just because of what she is. This isn't a compromise. If you want to become clan members, you'll have to accept that she and possibly other Kudlaks are clan members as much as you are."

Alexis pressed a hand against Caroline's arm. "We don't have a problem with that. We've seen that not all Kudlaks are evil." But most of them were, which meant that if they were sticking around, Alexis would keep an eye on this person. He wouldn't put Caroline and Jonas in danger and didn't care what Rowan had to say about it.

Rachel was one of the best fighters in their group, so even though it hurt to know that she could kick Boyd's ass anytime she wanted, it didn't make him feel too bad. Now that he was fighting Chris, though, he wanted to show Clay that he deserved his spot here. That meant putting everything he had into the fight, even though Chris was one of his best friends.

Chris had been a bit down since they'd arrived, probably because of Linda. Boyd wondered if he'd expected her to come with them. As far as he knew, the relationship between them hadn't been official, but they'd been close. It had to hurt to know that she'd chosen Cornelius over Chris, and Boyd wasn't quite sure how to deal with it. Should he ask Chris about her? Should he just tell him he was there whenever he needed him? Or should he ignore all of it and focus on his own problems?

Chris tried to punch him, and Boyd grabbed his wrist and twisted. He moved around Chris, placed his boot against Chris's ass, and pushed him forward. Chris almost lost balance, but he managed to stay on his feet and quickly turned around.

Now that they were the other way around, Boyd noticed a small group of people coming toward them. Rowan was talking to three people Boyd had never seen before, and he wondered if they were here to become part of the clan. They'd need many more people to fill all the houses in the village.

Boyd focused on the fight. He kicked at Chris's legs and managed to send him stumbling back, but Chris wasn't giving up. His jaw was set, and it was as if he was fighting someone he disliked. Maybe he was imagining that Boyd was

Cornelius. If it helped him work through his feelings, Boyd didn't have a problem with that.

His gaze caught on one of the people with Rowan. All three were extremely good-looking, but this guy was even more so. Boyd didn't think he'd ever seen anyone more beautiful than this man. His hair was dark blond and flopped in front of his eyes. Unfortunately, Boyd couldn't see what color they were from a distance, but their color didn't matter. What did matter was that he couldn't take his gaze away from the man, which gave Chris the opening he needed.

His punch landed straight on Boyd's nose. Boyd yelped and stumbled back, and Chris took the opportunity to swipe his legs from under him. Once again, Boyd landed in the dirt.

He stared at the sky, berating himself for getting distracted. He'd needed this win, dammit. He had to show Clay and Rowan that he belonged here and that they'd done a good thing by allowing him to come along. They wouldn't want to provide for him any longer if they realized he didn't want to do this and that he sucked at fighting.

"Everything okay?" a voice Boyd didn't recognize asked.

He blinked up at the sky one last time, then sat up to find the man he'd been staring at standing in front of him.

The man's head was cocked as he stared at Boyd. His two friends had stayed back with Rowan, who was talking to Clay and gesturing at them. Chris had a sheepish expression on his face, and when he offered Boyd his hand, Boyd took it and let his friend haul him to his feet.

"I really didn't think that punch would land," Chris explained.

"It wouldn't have if I hadn't been distracted."

"I don't know about that. I feel I'm becoming better at this," Chris said as he raised his arms to show Boyd his biceps.

Boyd rolled his eyes.

"He's right. I don't think you would have landed that

punch if he hadn't been distracted," the beautiful man said. His gaze moved to Boyd. "But getting distracted in a fight against a Kudlak is deadly. You're lucky this is just training."

Boyd shuffled his feet. He didn't want Clay and Rowan—or this guy—to feel that he wasn't good enough. He had no idea why, but he felt the need to impress him.

He cleared his throat. "I'm not usually this distracted."

"I don't know," Chris interjected. "You've been plenty distracted lately."

Boyd glared at him. Chris didn't understand what was happening here. Boyd didn't either, so he wasn't surprised. He just knew he wanted the new guy to think that he had his shit together.

"Can I take your friend's place?" the guy asked.

"You want to fight Boyd?"

The man nodded. "I think I could show you a few things that would help," he told Boyd.

Boyd rubbed his palms over his thighs. They were clammy, which was weird because he didn't have a reason to be nervous.

Except for the glint in the man's eyes and the peek of his fangs under his upper lip.

"You're a Krsnik."

The man nodded. "I'm Alexis."

"Boyd."

"I'm aware. Your friend gave me your name."

Boyd needed to stop behaving like an idiot. "Right. I'm only human, so I'm not sure it's fair to fight against you."

Alexis arched a brow. "Are you or aren't you a hunter?"

"I've been a hunter for years."

"Then you fought Kudlaks. They're as strong as Krsniks, if not more because the ones who hunt and hurt humans don't have a conscience. They don't hesitate to kill any hunter who goes against them, especially human hunters."

"I'm aware of that," Boyd said through gritted teeth.

Who did Alexis think he was? He was talking to Boyd as if Boyd had no idea what he was doing, and while he might be right in part, Boyd had survived many encounters with Kudlaks. He'd even killed a few of them, although never by himself.

Human hunters needed to hunt in pairs or groups. They weren't as strong as Kudlaks and Krsniks, and it could become dangerous in the blink of an eye. They always needed backup, and usually, Boyd hunted with Chris and Kendrick. As a trio, they were good at what they did. On their own, though, Boyd was very much aware of the fact that they wouldn't survive.

"Alexis and his friends are here to see if they could become part of our clan," Rowan explained from where he stood with the others. "Caroline and Alexis are hunters, so they know what they're doing. They can help you get better." He looked around. "All of you. I understand you have experience and have defeated Kudlaks before, but you must remember that you're only human."

Boyd grunted. "Fine. Let's see Alexis kick my ass."

Alexis grinned as if excited to show Boyd how much better he was. Boyd had no doubt that was true.

They got into position, and Boyd got ready to get hurt. He hoped Alexis would go easy on him and remember that he was human, but from the first punch, he realized that wouldn't be the case. Alexis would make him work for this.

So Boyd did. He'd wanted to show Clay and Rowan that he was a good hunter, and this was the perfect opportunity. He was fighting a Krsnik alone and didn't have Alexis's strength and speed. He also didn't have his experience, but then Alexis was probably decades older than he was. None of that mattered as Boyd defended himself from Alexis's attacks and tried to get at least a punch in.

He feigned to the left, and when he saw Alexis move that way, he almost whooped in victory. Instead, he quickly moved to the right to sweep Alexis's legs from under him. It worked, but Alexis wasn't going to go down easily. As he fell, he grabbed Boyd and twisted them so that Boyd ended up under him with Alexis straddling his hips.

That was the worst position they could end up in. Boyd didn't want Alexis to realize just how sexy he found him, so he quickly used his larger body to turn them back around. He slammed Alexis's back into the ground, and with his body covering Alexis's, they ended up pressed together and looking each other in the eyes.

Alexis was tiny under Boyd. Boyd was six foot two and well-built, with wide shoulders and strong arms. On the other hand, Alexis was around five foot six or seven and slight. Boyd was aware that didn't mean Alexis was weak, but he realized just how strong the Krsnik was when he pushed him away. Boyd had expected it, but he still couldn't resist the movement, and he ended up on his back again while Alexis scrambled to his feet.

For a moment, he and Alexis stared at each other. Something had happened, but Boyd had no idea what.

Alexis had gotten what he'd expected from this experience. He'd wanted to know if Boyd could hold his own against a Krsnik, and he'd found out that, yes, Boyd could. He was only human, so it would be easy for Alexis to kill him eventually, but that wasn't the important part of this experience.

No, the important part was that Boyd was Alexis's mate.

When he, his friends, and Rowan had walked up to the group training, Alexis's gaze had caught on Boyd immediately. He'd told himself it was because he'd always liked redheads, and Boyd was gorgeous. His hair was fiery red, his eyes green, and his pale skin was covered in freckles everywhere Alexis could see. They made Alexis want to lick all of them and maybe even count them, and the muscles Boyd had hidden under his t-shirt and pants didn't help the matter.

How Boyd looked wasn't why Alexis had offered to help him train. He'd wanted to feel Boyd under his touch, but part of him had also wanted to make sure Boyd could defend himself. He hadn't understood why he'd felt panicked at the thought that Boyd could be killed while hunting.

Now, he did.

He also understood why Boyd had been distracted before. Even though he was human, he probably felt drawn to Alexis. He couldn't feel the bond, but he could sense there was something between them. Even now, as they stared at each other, it was obvious that Boyd was waiting for something.

Alexis wanted nothing more than to straddle Boyd's body again and kiss him senseless. He wanted to bond with him, bite him and, drink his blood, link them together for the rest of their lives. They'd just met, but Alexis could see his future in Boyd's eyes.

It was nuts. This shouldn't be possible, even though they were mates. Alexis had always understood what finding your mate meant but hadn't realized it would be so *much*. He felt like his heart might explode, and at the same time, he wanted to scream.

"Alexis?" Rowan asked. "Everything all right?"

"I didn't hurt you, did I?" Boyd asked as he got to his feet.

Alexis shook his head. "I'm fine." The problem was that he didn't know what to do. Should he tell Boyd they were mates right here and now? He could get away with not telling him because Boyd was human, but was it the right thing to do? Alexis had no idea.

He'd always known that he might meet his mate, but he hadn't expected it to happen now. He wasn't prepared, and he had no idea how to deal with the feelings that having Boyd in front of him had created. He was terrified of making the wrong decision, yet at the same time, he wanted nothing more than to run away and hide.

That was what he did. He wasn't proud of it and knew he'd regret it, but he couldn't face Boyd right now. He couldn't face anyone. He didn't understand what was happening and needed a moment to wrap his mind around all of this, so he turned to rush off, anywhere, just away.

Jonas had hoped that Rowan would welcome them into his clan. Alexis would have been happy, too, but he'd been suspicious. Now, he wanted nothing more than for Rowan to offer him a place here. He couldn't leave, knowing that his mate was here and a hunter to boot. He needed to protect Boyd and make sure nothing happened to him. He had to kill any Kudlak who looked Boyd's way.

A hand grabbed Alexis's wrist and stopped his exit. Alexis half expected it to be Boyd, but instead, Jonas stood in front of him.

His eyes were wide, and his expression was worried. He raised both hands as he let go of Alexis as if he was afraid Alexis would attack him.

Alexis snorted. "I'm not going to punch you."

"Good. I wasn't sure, because your reaction was weird. What's going on? Did that guy do something to you?"

Alexis shook his head. "He didn't do anything."

"Are you sure? Because it didn't look like it. It's almost like you've seen a ghost." Jonas's eyes widened. "Is that what happened? Did you see a ghost?"

Alexis couldn't help but smile. He grabbed Jonas's neck and pulled him closer to press a kiss to his hair. "I didn't see a ghost. They don't exist."

Jonas pushed him away. "Let go. You're going to mess up my hair."

"I'm pretty sure everyone here is already half in love with you, so it doesn't matter that your hair is messy."

Alexis was joking, but the words still left a bitter aftertaste in his mouth. He didn't want everyone to be half in love with Jonas. He didn't want *Boyd* to be half in love with Jonas. Boyd was his mate. He should be half in love with him.

Alexis groaned. He'd just met Boyd, yet his mate was already messing with his head. How was he supposed to think about whether or not he and his friends should stay when the only thing he wanted to do was never leave this village again? He couldn't stay just because Boyd was here. He needed to make a rational decision but wasn't sure he could.

"Now you're making me worry," Jonas said. He looked back. "You want me to get Caroline?"

"I'm fine."

"You don't look fine. And you're not acting like you're fine. I didn't actually think the hunter did anything to you, but I'm starting to wonder. What's going on? You know you can talk to me."

Jonas and Caroline were the only people Alexis could talk to. They were his best friends and his family, and he wanted both of them to know what was happening.

But Jonas wanted to stay. Nothing would stop him from sticking around the village, and Alexis wanted them to make this decision rationally by considering all the pros and cons. If Jonas knew that Boyd was Alexis's mate, nothing would tear him away from this place anymore.

Alexis supposed that nothing would tear him away from the village, either. Now that he knew Boyd was here, it was too late. Rational or not, his entire being wanted to become a clan member, and there was nothing he could do about it.

He sighed and kicked a small rock with his foot. "I freaked out," he admitted.

"Yeah, everyone noticed you freaked out. One second, you

were staring at the guy, and the next, you were gone. Is it because he's your type? I know redheads do it for you." Jonas leaned closer. "Were you getting a boner? If so, you have nothing to be ashamed of. I mean, the guy is hot, even though I don't usually do redheads."

Alexis groaned. "Can you stop talking about boners and who you'd do or wouldn't do?"

"You know how to stop me from talking about this. Tell me what's happening."

"He's my mate, all right?"

Jonas gaped and stared at Alexis.

Alexis needed him to say something, but it looked like he was in shock. He wasn't the only one. Alexis hadn't expected to find his mate here, of all places, and he didn't know how to deal with it. Part of him wanted to rush back to Boyd and tell him everything, while the other part couldn't help but point out that he'd probably freak out Boyd if he did that. Boyd was human, and even though he knew about mates, he might not want to link his life to the life of a Krsnik.

"That's it," Jonas eventually said. "We're staying."

"We shouldn't make that decision lightly."

"I'm not making it lightly. I was going to stay whether you and Caroline wanted it or not. Now that I know you're sticking around, there's no reason not to tell you."

That hurt. "You were going to leave us?"

"I was hoping I wouldn't have to, but maybe. I don't want to lose you, but I can't live this life anymore. I want more than crappy apartments and horrible jobs. I want a real home and people who care about me."

"Caroline and I care about you."

Jonas smiled. "I know. I care about you, too, and if I can avoid it at all, I'm never leaving the two of you. I'm not made for the life you live, though. I'm not a hunter, and I never will be. I need more than my destiny of going out there and kicking Kudlak ass."

"And you think you've found it here?"

Jonas grinned. "I *know* I have, and so have you."

CHAPTER THREE

Boyd was distracted. That was nothing new, but the direction his thoughts had taken was. Instead of obsessing over how he didn't want to be a hunter or how he wasn't a good fighter, he couldn't stop thinking about the newcomer. As he poked at his breakfast, he once again wondered what had happened yesterday to send Alexis running. Had Boyd been that bad at fighting? Did Alexis think there was no hope for him?

But if that was why, he wouldn't have run. He hadn't had a reason to run as far as Boyd had seen. He'd even come back after a while, trailed by one of the other people he'd arrived with. They'd obviously been close, and Boyd had needed to work hard not to scowl at the cute, short guy who had to be a close friend of Alexis. Even now, he wished he'd pulled the guy away to take his place by Alexis's side.

Except that wasn't Boyd's place. His place was at the village, doing his best to protect his new clan and the rest of the world from Kudlaks. What happened yesterday shouldn't matter. *Alexis* shouldn't matter.

But he did, very much so. Boyd didn't understand why he wanted the Krsnik to think well of him and view him as a good fighter. At the very least, he wanted Alexis to know that he could take care of himself. He'd faced Kudlaks before, and he'd gotten out alive. That meant he wasn't that bad, right?

Alexis was Boyd's type, but Boyd wasn't trying to seduce him. He didn't think he'd have a chance with the guy. Alexis was too pretty, strong, and focused to want someone like him.

Boyd could hope, but he wouldn't be surprised when that hope crashed and burned.

Just like he had yesterday. He'd gotten his ass kicked by too many people, and it hurt—and not just physically. Boyd hated feeling like he didn't belong, but there was no ignoring it. He didn't fit in with the hunters, but that didn't mean he wasn't going to fight to stay.

He expected Clay or Rowan to visit him eventually. They probably had better things to do than to kick him out of the clan at the moment, and Boyd wanted to take advantage of every second he had here. He had a training session again this afternoon, but he had time to do things around the house this morning.

It looked good. He'd cleaned everything inside as soon as he'd moved in, and thankfully, the furniture and the house were sturdy. There wouldn't need to be any construction work inside, but the yard needed a little love, and that was Boyd's specialty.

Once he was done with breakfast and had placed his dirty dishes in the sink after rinsing them, he headed upstairs. He put on an old pair of sweats and a thick sweater, ready for a morning outside.

The cold air hit his face as soon as he opened the front door. It hadn't snowed yet, but it would soon. He wanted to take advantage of the lack of snow to settle everything in the yard and make sure it survived until next spring. Thankfully, the old owners of the house had kept a lot of yard tools in the shed behind the house, so Boyd was set to do whatever he needed this morning.

He lost himself in work. It had always been like that, ever since he'd started working with his father. He'd been a landscaper, and Boyd had loved going to work with him. It wasn't always a quiet job, but it was peaceful, and it allowed Boyd to settle his mind and not obsess over his everyday problems.

When he was a kid, those problems were his homework and what he'd eat for dinner. Now, he had bigger things to worry about, and sometimes it took his breath away. He'd always thought that once he was an adult, he'd know what to do, but he'd realized a while ago that no one knew what they were doing, even when they were firmly into adulthood.

Working in the yard made him miss his father, but he knew better than to reach out to him. Boyd's parents had wanted him to stay after Amy died, and Boyd had tried for a while. He'd felt unsettled and full of thoughts of revenge, so it hadn't lasted long. He hated that they'd lost him along with Amy, but at least they still had one of their kids. Evan had stayed behind and was the only one Boyd was still in contact with.

He didn't like being unable to call his parents, but he knew that if he heard their voices, he'd run straight home, and he couldn't afford that. He still had work to do, and not just when it came to Kudlaks.

But maybe now that he had a place to call home and he was settling down, he could call them. At the very least, he could reassure them that he was all right. He was still a hunter, so the possibility that he'd die was high, but at least they'd know he'd been happy in the meantime.

He was. Boyd had never thought he'd be happy again after his sister had been killed, especially not such a quiet happiness. He might be lonely, but it was easy to settle down now that he wasn't living in an abandoned warehouse with people he despised. If he could live the rest of his life here, tending to the yard, it would be perfect.

It was still impossible for him to wrap his mind around the fact that he had all of this. He'd known what he was doing when he'd left his parents behind. He'd been thirsty for revenge, and in a way, he still was. But he'd realized a while ago that no matter how many Kudlaks he killed, it would never feel like it was enough. That was the only thing he could focus on for many years.

Not anymore. He didn't want to hunt because he'd never liked it. He'd done it because he felt he had to, but now, he knew the truth. His anger and sadness at his sister's death would never leave him. The feelings had faded somewhat, but they'd always be there, and he had to learn to live with them. Hopefully, having a clan and a place to call home would help him with that.

That wouldn't be useful if people expected him to continue being a hunter. He should probably talk to Clay and Rowan and be honest with them, but a big part of him was terrified that if he did, they'd kick him out, and he'd lose everything. He didn't think he could live with that. He might never have expected to have a home again, but he didn't want to lose it.

Someone cleared their throat behind him, causing him to jump. He turned to glance at the person, only to freeze when he saw Alexis.

Boyd scrambled to his feet. Alexis was outside the fence that ran around the house, looking out of place. Boyd was the only person around, so it was clear that Alexis was there to see him.

Boyd had no idea why.

They stared at each other for a moment. The air between them felt like it was charged, and Boyd wanted nothing more than to reach out for Alexis. He was terrified of what Alexis would do if he tried, so he kept his hands to himself. He'd already gotten his ass kicked by the Krsnik once. He wasn't looking forward to it happening a second time.

Alexis cleared his throat again. He shuffled his feet, which wasn't a gesture Boyd had expected to see from this man. It made him realize that, for some reason, Alexis was uncomfortable. Boyd doubted it was because of him, but maybe he could try to make things more comfortable for both of them.

"Are you looking for someone?" he asked.

Alexis stopped moving, but he was still staring. It was kind of awkward and made Boyd want to turn and run back into the house. He'd look like an idiot if he did so, though, so he stayed where he was and waited.

Alexis cleared his throat a third time, then scowled. Boyd might have been offended by the rudeness of the expression if he hadn't suspected it was directed at Alexis himself.

"I am looking for someone," Alexis admitted.

"Who is it? I can tell you where to find them."

"I already have."

Boyd was staring at Alexis as if he didn't understand what Alexis was saying.

Maybe he didn't. Alexis felt like he was making a mess out of this.

He wasn't sure what he was doing here. He still hadn't decided if he should tell Boyd they were mates, but he'd wanted to see him, and it had been easy to find him. Jonas already seemed to know where everyone in the village lived, and he'd given Alexis precise directions.

They'd spent the night at the village. Jonas had acted as if it was a given, but Alexis was still wary, and he thought Caroline felt the same. They were waiting for the other shoe to drop, while Jonas was already focused on his future. Jonas had been in as soon as Rowan told him that he would welcome anyone who wanted to help their clan grow. It was as if he'd grown up here and had always belonged, and Alexis was in awe.

He didn't understand how Jonas could feel that way. These people were strangers, and even if he trusted them the way Jonas clearly did, Alexis would never have been able to be as relaxed as his friend was. It would take time for him to truly consider this place home.

Maybe having a mate would help.

Alexis almost cleared his throat a fourth time but caught himself and stopped. He waited for Boyd to answer, but Boyd was still staring.

"I was looking for you," Alexis eventually said.

Boyd blinked. "That's what I thought you'd said, but I'm not sure I understand. Why would you be looking for me?"

The words *because you're my mate* didn't burst out of Alexis's mouth, but it was a close thing. Alexis bit his lower lip and told himself to calm down. He didn't want to send Boyd running. He had no idea what he wanted from his mate, but it wasn't to see the back of his head as he ran for the hills.

"I wanted to apologize," Alexis explained.

He wished Boyd would invite him inside the house. He was curious to see the place where his mate lived, and he hated making a spectacle of himself. Even though he didn't think anyone was watching them, he could have sworn he could feel people's gazes on his back. Maybe Jonas and Caroline were hidden in the bushes waiting to see what would happen. They were excited that he'd met his mate. Now that he'd had some time to wrap his mind around it, Alexis felt the same way, but it only added to the confusion.

He'd never actually *wanted* to meet his mate. He'd known it could happen, but he'd been busy surviving and killing Kudlaks. He'd never allowed himself to wonder what he'd do when he met his mate, but he should have. He wouldn't be as lost as he was now if he had. He didn't know what to do.

"Why would you want to apologize to me?" Boyd asked. "If it's because you kicked my ass yesterday, you don't have to. I'm used to it, and it was training."

"It's not that." Alexis paused. "Well, I do apologize for throwing you around. I shouldn't have asked to fight you."

Boyd leaned against the fence. "Because you're a Krsnik, and I'm human?"

44

"Yes. Our fight wasn't fair."

"But fights with Kudlaks aren't fair, either. You told me that yesterday." Boyd shook his head. "There's nothing for you to apologize for. You tried to help me, and you kicked my ass. I'm not surprised you did, and I don't expect anything from you."

He doesn't know we're mates. Alexis told himself that again so he wouldn't feel hurt by the fact that Boyd was dismissing him. He thought that Alexis was just here to apologize before leaving. He didn't know how important he was to Alexis, and Alexis wasn't sure he could find words to explain.

But he wasn't done with his apology.

"I also wanted to explain why I ran off." That would only work if he told Boyd they were mates, but maybe it was the best thing to do. Right now, it was the *only* thing Alexis could think of doing.

"That was a bit weird," Boyd said. He was smiling, so Alexis wasn't offended.

"I'm not usually that weird. Jonas is the weird one in our little family."

"The guy you arrived with, right?"

"Yes. Jonas and Caroline are my best friends and have been my family for decades."

"And you guys want to move here?"

"Possibly. We wanted to see what this place was about. We didn't think there were any more Krsniks out there, but I'm glad to see we were wrong."

"I mean, I've only met the three of you and Rowan until now, but hopefully, other Krsniks will hear about this place and decide they want to become part of our clan."

"Clans need to grow," Alexis agreed.

"I guess so. It's still weird to think that all of this is real."

And Alexis was about to drop massive news over this mess. He needed to stop wasting time because it would only make things worse. He just had to be honest with Boyd. There was no way to know how Boyd would react to the news, but there was only one way to find out. Alexis wasn't sure he was ready, but that didn't matter. He needed to do this.

"I understand why you feel that way. My friends and I have been on our own for so long that it's strange to believe we could find a home here."

Boyd grinned. "Exactly. I'm sure other people feel the same way, but it feels like a dream, you know? It's good to have you on board. We need the help when it comes to hunting."

"We'll help," Alexis promised.

Boyd continued staring at him. He was probably waiting for Alexis to either continue talking or leave. Alexis was rooted in place, and he couldn't seem to make his mouth work. It was ridiculous and made him look like a fool, which was the only reason he managed to get unstuck. He didn't want his mate to think he was an idiot, which, from Boyd's expression, was precisely what was happening.

"I apologize," he said. "I wanted you to know I was sorry for running away from you. I had a good reason to do so, though."

"Was I that bad at fighting?"

The self-deprecation in Boyd's voice made Alexis grit his teeth. He didn't like the way his mate talked about himself, but there wasn't much he could do. Maybe in time, Boyd would start thinking better of himself. Alexis would tell him how wonderful he was every day if that was what he needed to do.

But first, he had to get Boyd to agree to give them a chance. That wouldn't happen if he wasn't honest.

"It wasn't your ability at fighting," he said as calmly as he could. "But while we were rolling around in the dirt, your scent hit me."

He looked up at Boyd. He'd expected and hoped Boyd

would get the hint, but he didn't say anything. He just waited for Alexis to continue.

Alexis did. "When I smelled you, I realized you were my mate. I didn't expect it, and my first instinct was to run. I'm sorry I did, and I want you to know it won't happen again."

Boyd snorted and looked around. "This is a prank, right? Who put you up to it? Kendrick or Chris?"

Well, damn. Alexis's mate thought that Alexis's confession was a prank. How was Alexis supposed to convince differently?

Boyd expected one of his friends to jump out of the bushes or something like that. They had to be around watching, right? They'd want to see Boyd's reaction to the prank.

It was a bit cruel. Boyd had never told his friends how lonely he felt, but he suspected they knew anyway. Most of the hunters felt that way most of the time, although that might be changing soon.

But Boyd couldn't see his friends. He frowned and turned his attention back to Alexis, who was still standing there. He looked a little pale, and he was gaping at Boyd.

"Do you need to sit down? You shouldn't have agreed to prank me if you couldn't do it," Boyd said as he gestured at an opening in the fence. He'd have to fix it, but it came in handy for now.

"It's not a prank," Alexis croaked. "I'm not lying to you. You're my mate."

Boyd told himself not to believe him, even though, from Alexis's expression, it appeared he was telling the truth. It didn't make sense. Alexis was a gorgeous man and a Krsnik. He needed someone strong who could keep up with him when it came to hunting Kudlaks. Boyd was the opposite of that. He didn't suck as a hunter — if he did, he would have died a while ago—but he couldn't say he was good, either. He wasn't sure he'd have a place in the clan once the others realized just how badly he wanted not to continue hunting, but hunting was Alexis's life.

No one in their right mind would believe they were mates. Boyd certainly didn't, and he didn't like this prank. It hurt, but he didn't want to blame Alexis for it. His friends had to be behind it, and he'd make sure to tell them how fucked up this was as soon as he got his hands on them.

"I can see that you still don't believe me," Alexis continued. "What do I have to do to convince you it's the truth? You don't know me, so you don't know that I wouldn't lie to you. This is a problem of trust. Can't you feel the bond between us?"

"I'm human. I don't feel mate bonds," Boyd said, pointing out while at the same time praying Alexis was telling the truth. He was a disaster, but maybe he was a disaster with a mate.

Boyd had no idea what to do with a mate and even less idea of what to do with Alexis. He was out of Boyd's league by miles, and if Boyd could see it, everyone could. People would wonder why the two of them were together.

Alexis sighed. "I'm not lying," he said quietly. "I smelled you yesterday, and when I realized you were my mate, I got overwhelmed. I still don't know if I can trust Rowan and the rest of the clan, but I was willing to take a chance on them because of Jonas. Then you barged into my life, and you're giving me one more reason to stay. Jonas has already decided that none of us was leaving."

"Is he your leader?" Boyd's voice sounded rough.

Alexis snorted. "He gets lost even with a map and can't fight his way out of a wet paper bag. He has the common sense of a potato. He'd be a disaster as a leader."

Alexis's words made Boyd smile. They hadn't been said

with heat or anger. Alexis was just describing how one of his best friends was, but he wasn't scorning Jonas for any of it.

"He does sound like he wouldn't be great at leading you."

"He wouldn't be." Alexis took a step forward. "How can I convince you I'm not lying? I don't expect anything from you, and I certainly don't expect you to want to be with me just because I'm your mate. I just need you to know what's going on and to accept it. I need you to *believe* it."

Boyd swallowed. He was so close to Alexis that he could touch him if he raised his hand. He desperately wanted to, but he was also terrified. He didn't want to send Alexis running, and he had no idea how to make sure that wouldn't happen.

He wanted to believe Alexis. He just wasn't sure if he could.

"I don't think repeating it will help much," he said. "I guess that maybe once I accept that neither Kendrick nor Chris are around, I'll start believing you. It's just impossible, you know?"

"I don't. Why is it impossible for you to be my mate?"

Boyd looked down at his hands. He was clutching the fence and stopping himself from reaching for Alexis. Even if they were mates, there was no way to know if Alexis would want to be touched. Maybe he was just here to explain what was going on and disappear from his life. Maybe he wanted to tell him to stay away.

That didn't make sense, but very little in Boyd's life made sense at the moment.

"Because I'm not the kind of guy who gets that lucky," Boyd murmured. "I don't have a job and nothing to offer. I don't understand why we're mates. There has to be a mistake."

"What if there isn't? How would you feel about it?"

Boyd had to look up. "I'd be happy. Who wouldn't want a mate like you?"

Alexis nodded as if he'd expected that answer. "Then you better start being happy, because I'm not lying. You're my mate, Boyd. I smelled you yesterday, and there isn't any mistake. You belong to me, and I belong to you." He pressed his lips together. "As long as you're willing, of course."

For the first time, Boyd allowed himself to hope. Alexis was cute, strong, and he wasn't cruel or mean from what Boyd had seen so far. He seemed like a good person, and they had at least one thing in common. They were both hunters, even though they belonged to two different species.

"I'm really your mate?" he asked.

Alexis didn't seem annoyed that he had to repeat himself again. "You're really my mate," he confirmed.

Boyd believed it this time. Alexis didn't have a reason to lie, and Kendrick and Chris were nowhere to be seen. That meant that Alexis was telling the truth and that he and Boyd belonged together.

What the fuck?

Boyd chuckled. He had to hold himself up against the fence to avoid falling on his ass. "I'm going to be honest and tell you that I have no idea what to do with this. Are we supposed to agree that we're going to bond? Or maybe decide that we'll only do it in a few years? What's the next step?"

Alexis's shoulders slumped just a bit as if he'd finally let himself relax. Boyd hadn't noticed how tense Alexis was before, but now, he could see it, and he wanted nothing more than to drag him into his arms.

In all of his past relationships, it had been his job to comfort the person he was with. He was usually bigger than them, and even when his sister had died, he'd had to comfort his boyfriend at the time. Boyd's ex had cried on Boyd's shoulder for hours, but when Boyd had needed to talk about what had happened, he'd told him he didn't want to because it hurt too much. Boyd was used to that kind of behavior, so he hadn't been offended. The relationship had ended soon after, anyway.

But something told him that things wouldn't be that way with Alexis. Apparently, Boyd was his mate, which meant he was supposed to know how to be there for him. Maybe Boyd would finally have someone who cared about him and his feelings.

"I don't know the next step," Alexis admitted. "It's not just because of you. I don't know what will happen next in my life. Jonas wants to stay, so I think we'll stick around, but I don't know what it means for our relationship."

It hurt a bit to realize that Alexis was only staying for his friend, but Boyd wasn't about to say that out loud. Alexis hadn't had to tell him they were mates. He could have kept the news to himself and left the village, and Boyd would have never found out.

"I guess we have a lot of thinking and talking to do," he said.

Oh, goody.

Alexis didn't have answers for Boyd. Maybe he should have thought about it before finding his mate and telling him they belonged together, but it hadn't occurred to him. Part of him worried that Boyd would refuse to see him after what had happened yesterday, and he'd needed to get it over with. He had, and he still didn't know what the fuck was happening in his life.

He'd never hoped to find his mate, but Boyd was standing before him. He liked what he'd seen of him. From the fight yesterday and a few conversations he'd had with other members of the clan, he knew that Boyd was strong, resilient, and a hard worker. He wasn't the best fighter, but he was a hunter and good enough to defend himself from Kudlaks.

Alexis wanted to ask why Boyd had become a hunter. He wanted to know how Boyd had learned that Kudlaks were real. Every human knew about shifters and most paranormal creatures by now, but there were still things that went bump in the night that humans hadn't confronted yet. Kudlaks and Krsniks were two of those things. Only a few humans knew about them, and most of them found out by accident. That was good, because it meant there was no mass hysteria about Kudlaks, and people weren't hiding in their homes, and it gave Alexis and the others the anonymity they needed.

Usually, it wasn't a good thing when humans became hunters. Alexis had crossed paths with a few of them over the decades, and their stories had always been sad. Most of the time, they'd lost someone dear to them, like a parent, sibling, or maybe a partner. Once they found out it had been Kudlaks, they wanted revenge and fell into the hunter's life.

It wasn't an easy life. It had never been, even for Alexis. He'd lost his entire clan and the people he'd been the closest to. He didn't have any family left. He only had Jonas and Caroline, and he thanked fate every day for them.

But now he had a chance at having a mate, and he wasn't going to waste it. He might not have a clue what he was doing, but he'd find out. Alexis didn't do relationships, but he was going to have to start. He'd never bothered before because it didn't fit well with his lifestyle. He didn't want to have to explain to anyone why he spent the night prowling the city. He didn't want to explain the bloodstains, emergencies, or why he lived with Jonas and Caroline.

He wouldn't have to explain anything to Boyd because Boyd already knew. Hell, Boyd would probably be fighting by his side the next time they found a Kudlak.

And that brought up an entirely new set of problems. How was Alexis supposed to hunt with his mate? He was already freaked out at the thought of anything happening to Boyd, and they weren't even together. How could he stand next to Boyd and possibly watch him get hurt?

Maybe Alexis should talk to Clay and Rowan about it. They were mates and bonded, yet they fought together. Alexis had a hard time seeing that happening for him and Boyd, but only time would tell.

"So you're really staying?" Boyd asked.

Alexis nodded. "I didn't expect us to stick around, but Jonas is bent on making this place his new home, and neither Caroline nor I are willing to leave him behind. There's also you to think about now."

"Not if you really want to go. I won't stop you if you hate this place," Boyd quickly said.

Alexis glared at him. "You're more important than me not liking the village."

"Not really. I'm just a guy."

Did he not understand? "You're not just a guy. You're my mate, and that means everything to shifters, Krsniks included. I don't know what's going to happen between us, but I won't find out if I don't stick around and give us a chance." Alexis frowned. "Unless you don't want this?"

Maybe that was why Boyd was saying he wouldn't mind if Alexis left. Maybe he didn't want Alexis to stick around.

Alexis knew next to nothing about his mate, but he needed that to change.

"I guess it's harder for me to understand since I'm human," Boyd said. "But I'm not going to try to change your mind if you're convinced of what you're doing."

"I am."

"And I think it's good that you're not staying just because of me. That way, you won't resent me if you change your mind."

It was as if Boyd couldn't accept that he was Alexis's mate. He was apologizing and trying to keep Alexis happy, but that wasn't how bonds between mates worked. Sure, Boyd wanted to make Alexis happy, but the same went for Alexis.

Boyd was his future, and he *needed* him to be happy.

He finally walked in through the opening in the fence. He made a mental note that he'd have to fix it, but that wasn't why he was here today. He moved toward Boyd, smiling at the way his mate watched him with wide eyes. Boyd hadn't expected this, and Alexis enjoyed surprising his mate. He liked how Boyd looked when he stared at him as he moved closer, and he wanted this to continue for years.

"I want something to be clear," Alexis said once he reached Boyd.

"I'm listening," Boyd said with a squeak.

"You're my mate. There's no mistake, and I'm not angry about it. Physically, you're the kind of guy I usually go for. I love redheads, and I like being with guys who are taller than me. Everything else will be just as well suited to me as I am to you."

"You like redheads?" Boyd asked in a small voice.

It made Alexis wonder if some people had made fun of him for his hair and freckles. If so, he'd hunt them down. "I love it. Even if you were shorter and scrawny with black hair, it wouldn't change the fact that we're mates. I'm not going to change my mind about being with you, and I won't resent you for making me stay, because you're not. It's a decision I'm making, and while you play a big part in it, I wouldn't stay if I didn't think it was the right thing to do. I need you to stop thinking that I'm going to change my mind about you. I realize you don't know me, but eventually, you'll realize how serious I am about all of this. I just need you to give me a chance."

Boyd nodded eagerly. "I can do that. I want to do it."

Alexis grinned. "Good."

He knew that by smiling like this, he exposed his fangs. He needed Boyd to see them and not be afraid of them, so he kept an eye on his mate's reaction.

Boyd's focus dropped to the fangs instantly, and he swallowed heavily.

Alexis might have been worried if he also hadn't licked his lips. It looked like Boyd wanted to kiss Alexis, and Alexis was all for that.

He twisted his fingers into Boyd's sweater and pulled him closer. Boyd had to lean down to kiss Alexis, which wasn't a great feeling, but Alexis would get used to it. He didn't usually kiss the guys he was with, so it had never been a problem, but that was all in the past now.

Boyd's lips were soft, and he yielded instantly. He opened his mouth, allowing Alexis in. Alexis was surprised that Boyd gave him so much control, but maybe he shouldn't be. If fate had put them together, it meant they were perfectly suited for each other. It might take them some time to work things out, but eventually, they would.

Boyd cradled Alexis into his arms, and even though Alexis was the better fighter between them, the gesture made him feel protected and safe. It wasn't a feeling he'd often experienced since he'd lost his clan, but he was home.

And he was never leaving.

CHAPTER FOUR

Boyd caught Kendrick's fist with his hand. He twisted his body, trying to move behind his friend. Kendrick knew him well, though, and he moved with him. Boyd swore, and Kendrick grinned at him, no doubt happy that he'd managed to anticipate Boyd's move.

"You're going to have to try harder than that," he teased.

Boyd knew he should, but his heart wasn't into it. How was he supposed to focus on fighting and training when he couldn't stop thinking about Alexis? Maybe he would have been able to if he enjoyed hunting and wanted to continue being a hunter, but that wasn't the case.

Boyd couldn't imagine anything better than staying at home while Alexis went on hunts and welcoming him when he came back. Of course, he'd be terrified that something would happen to his mate, but Alexis knew what he was doing better than most people here. He'd been born to hunt Kudlaks, which showed in every movement he made, even when he was resting. On the other hand, Boyd felt clunky and like if he wasn't careful, his head would roll.

It would. He couldn't afford to be distracted when he fought Kudlaks. Thankfully, he hadn't been sent on a hunt yet, but eventually, he would be. When he was, he'd have to be careful, if anything so he could come back to Alexis.

He didn't have a choice. It was either fight or be kicked out of the clan and village, and he couldn't lose the only place he'd been able to call home in many years. He'd finally found a place where he belonged and wasn't giving it up.

But did he really belong here?

That was a question he didn't have an answer to. He wanted to say he did, but everyone here was a hunter. Everyone wanted to get rid of Kudlaks and avenge the loved ones they'd lost to them. Boyd wanted that, too, but even more, he wanted to be happy, and hunting didn't make him happy.

His sister would have been angry to see the life he lived and the man he'd become. She wouldn't have wanted him to lose years of his life running after the person who had killed her. Boyd would never be able to talk to her again and ask her for sure, but he'd known Amy as well as he knew himself. If she'd been able to see him, she would have yelled at him to stop being an idiot.

Maybe that was what he should do.

He was distracted, but thankfully, he still noticed how Kendrick leaned on one of his legs. That meant he was about to use the other one to hit Boyd, but Boyd caught him in time. He quickly stepped backward as Kendrick tried to swipe his legs from under him. He crouched and grabbed Kendrick's ankle, then turned his leg so that Kendrick had to go along with the movement if he didn't want to get hurt. He twisted in the air, and his other leg buckled under him when Boyd kicked at it. Kendrick fell face first flat on the ground, and Boyd quickly climbed onto his back. He grabbed one of Kendrick's hands and had to fight him for the second one, but eventually, he pulled both of them behind his back and locked his wrists in one of his hands, pushing him down harder.

"You win," Kendrick yelped.

Boyd still waited for a second longer before climbing off his friend. Kendrick rolled onto his back and glared at Boyd, but he wasn't actually angry. This was what they did. They trained, went on hunts, and killed as many Kudlaks as possible. It should be enough for Boyd.

It wasn't.

Boyd offered Kendrick his hand, and even though he didn't like any of this, it felt good to be the one who'd won for once. He'd needed it, and he grinned at Kendrick only to get another glare. Kendrick knocked their shoulders together once he was on his feet, and Boyd laughed.

"You don't have to be so smug," Kendrick complained.

"I'm not smug. It just feels good."

"I guess you needed the win after getting your ass kicked so many times."

It was Boyd's turned to glare. "Did you really have to remind me of that?"

Kendrick laughed. "I guess not. Sorry."

He wasn't sorry at all, but this was how they were. They were best friends and teased each other, and Boyd wouldn't change that for anything in the world.

This was another reason he didn't want to stop being a hunter. If he had to leave the village, he'd lose Kendrick and Chris, and that wasn't something he was willing to let happen. They were his best friends, two of the few people he truly cared about, and he'd already lost too much. He was never getting his sister back, but he could keep his chosen brothers.

"That was good," Clay said as he clasped Boyd's shoulder.

Boyd tried not to look too happy with Clay's praise. He had to appear like he knew what he was doing, dammit.

Clay stepped to the side with Boyd while Rachel and Chris stepped in the middle of their makeshift training ring. Boyd grabbed a bottle of water and went to lean against one of the houses, hoping Clay would get the hint.

He should have known better.

Clay never left his side. He leaned against the same wall, and while he was watching the fight, Boyd knew his attention was on him. It made him nervous, and he wasn't sure how to behave. Should he say something? Maybe ask Clay what he needed? That would be rude, right?

"How are you finding the village?" Clay eventually asked.

It wasn't the question Boyd had expected, but at least Clay was saying something.

"I like it. It's quiet and peaceful, and it already feels like home."

Clay nodded. "I know what you're saying. I guess that for guys like us, it's hard to find a place to call home. We've been on the move for too long."

"It's certainly better than the warehouse."

Clay laughed. "Anything would be better than the warehouse, especially with Cornelius hanging around like a giant bat. Really, though. How are you doing? I've been watching you and know you were out of sorts for a while. Then that stuff with Alexis happened a few days ago, and I can see things have shifted further."

Boyd didn't know if Alexis had told anyone about their bond. Boyd hadn't, but not because he didn't want people to know about it. He just had no idea what it meant yet.

He hadn't been avoiding Alexis. Alexis knew where he lived, so he'd be able to find him if he wanted to talk. Alexis and his friends were settling down, and Boyd didn't want to be a bother. When Alexis was ready, he'd come to Boyd.

Hopefully.

Boyd couldn't stop thinking about the kiss they'd shared. He wanted more, but he didn't think he could ask for it until they decided their next step. Boyd needed to stay at the village if he wanted a relationship with Alexis, which meant being a hunter.

He cleared his throat. "I'm fine. It was just a lot to take in."

Clay slowly nodded. Boyd was pretty sure he didn't believe him, but he doubted Clay would say anything about it. They were close, but not that close.

"What did you want to do before?" Clay asked, surprising Boyd.

He had no idea where that question was coming from.

"You mean before becoming a hunter?"

"Yeah. I wanted to be a lawyer."

Boyd laughed. "I can't see you being a lawyer."

"Neither can I, but I'm a much different man than I was back then. What about you?"

Boyd looked down at his feet. "I always thought I'd go into business with my father. He's a landscaper and does a lot of yard work."

"That's why you've been working so hard on your yard?"

"Yeah. It reminds me of him."

Clay hummed. "Well, you don't live in the warehouse anymore. You could contact your family."

"Have you contacted yours?"

Clay grinned. "Busted. It's hard when you know you'd be putting them in danger, isn't it?"

"They already lost my sister. I don't want them to be afraid they might lose me, too."

"Haven't they lost you in a way, though? I'm not saying you need to contact them or anything like that, but maybe think about it."

"Only if you do."

"I *have* been thinking about it. I want them to meet my mate. I want them to see what we're building together and how hard we're working to keep people safe."

Boyd had no doubt that Clay's family would be happy to see him again. He knew Clay had lost his parents and two sisters to Kudlaks, but he still had a few uncles, aunts, and his grandparents. Maybe they could become part of the village.

But they weren't hunters, and Boyd knew that to be part of the clan, he needed to be one.

"Ready?"

That was the first thing Rowan said when Alexis opened the door of the house he shared with Jonas and Caroline.

Alexis grinned. "I'm always ready to hunt."

"I don't know how you do it," Jonas complained from his spot on the couch behind Alexis. "All that gore and blood. I'd much rather stay at home on the couch."

"You stay here and watch your movie. We'll keep you safe," Alexis said, making sure to coo his words.

Jonas turned to glare at him and threw a pillow at him. Alexis caught it and threw it back, hitting him straight in the face. Jonas yelped and made a scene of rubbing his nose, but there was no way he was in pain.

Caroline pushed past Alexis to join Rowan on the porch. She had a no-nonsense expression that told Alexis it was time to stop joking around and follow Rowan to whatever hunt he'd decided to go on tonight.

Alexis wasn't surprised. Rowan was testing them to see if they would be a good fit with the other hunters and him, and Alexis hoped they would be. Now that he'd found Boyd, he wasn't planning on going anywhere, which meant that being told he wasn't a good fit would be a problem. He needed Rowan to like him and want him and the others to stay, and he'd do whatever he had to in order to make that happen.

After saying goodbye to Jonas, Alexis and Caroline followed Rowan down the porch steps. They joined a few human hunters waiting for them, including Clay, Rowan's mate. Alexis had seen him earlier today when he'd been training the hunters, but he'd stayed away because Boyd had been there. He hadn't wanted to distract his mate or catch the eye of anyone.

The only people he'd told about Boyd were Jonas and Caroline. Both of them had been happy for him, but since he didn't know how Rowan and the rest of his clan would take the news, he'd decided to keep it to himself. Boyd knew them better, so he should decide when he was ready to tell them. In the meantime, Alexis was fine keeping this to the people he trusted the most.

"I got news of a Kudlak nest not far from here," Rowan said.

"News from who?" Caroline asked.

"The council. They'd been keeping an eye on the news and an ear open, and since the enforcers answer to them, they usually find out about attacks before anyone else. They're not entirely sure it's Kudlaks, but they sent a team of enforcers, and they almost didn't make it out alive. That's why they contacted me."

Caroline nodded. Alexis suspected he knew what she was thinking. He didn't like working for the council any more than she did, but if this was how things needed to go, it was how they would go. It was a compromise, and it meant they'd be allowed to stay with the clan.

"How are we getting there?" Caroline asked, looking around.

None of them were standing next to a vehicle, but maybe they could walk there.

"They're sending a Nix to shimmer us back and forth."

"It would be easier if we could get a few Nix to move here with us," Clay pointed out.

"I'm working on it," Rowan promised.

The way he looked at Clay made Alexis look away. Clearly those two cared for each other, and he wondered if the same would happen to him and Boyd. He wanted to say yes, but what did he know?

Boyd was his mate, and Alexis had to remember that. He wasn't just a guy Alexis had met. He was Alexis's future, and he seemed to want this as much as Alexis.

A Nix appeared a few feet away, and Alexis took a moment to observe him. Why did he have pink hair and so many tattoos?

Clay groaned. "You again? The council said they were sending an enforcer."

The Nix glared. "What, I'm not good enough for you?"

"I think that what Clay is saying is that you're not a fighter," Rowan interjected, clearly trying to keep the bickering to a minimum.

The Nix raised his arms to show his biceps. "I'm strong."

"I have no doubt that you are, but Kudlaks are dangerous, especially when they nest. I don't want anything to happen to you."

That seemed to do the trick, and the Nix's expression softened. "I have orders to stay as far away from the nest as possible. My mate would kick my ass if he knew I'd gone anywhere close to it. Actually, he's going to kick my ass anyway because he told me not to do this, and I came anyway."

"He's going to kill us," Clay muttered. "Everyone, this is Nysys. Nysys, you already know the hunters. This is Caroline and Alexis. They're Krsniks."

Nysys's eyes widened. "Like Rowan and Emery?"

Alexis had no idea who Emery was. "Like Rowan," he confirmed.

Nysys clapped. "That's so neat. Will you have time to answer a few questions later?"

Clay mouthed *say no* from behind Nysys, and Alexis suspected it would be better if he took that warning to heart. "We'll see what happens during the hunt, all right?"

Nysys pouted. "Everyone here is so boring."

He held out his hands, and everyone gathered around him. Alexis clasped his shoulder, but he barely had time to wonder if the touch was firm enough. Nysys had already shimmered them away.

They appeared in an empty parking lot. When Alexis looked around, he saw an abandoned grocery store and knew that was where the nest was. It made sense. Kudlaks were like Krsniks, and while they needed blood to survive, they could also do so on human food. They'd need food because killing too many humans for their blood would put a spotlight on them and on the place they called home.

"I changed my mind," Nysys whispered. "I'm going to go back home and pick you up when you're done. This place is creepy."

"We'll be fine," Rowan promised him.

Alexis took out his knives, ready to fight. This was in his blood, what he'd been born to do and what he'd done since he was old enough to hold a knife. He wasn't worried about the fight.

That was until he remembered that he had someone to come home to.

He never had before and didn't know how to deal with it. He didn't want Boyd to be hurt, which meant he needed to go home to him.

Dammit. This was more complicated than he'd expected. He supposed he shouldn't be surprised. Feelings rarely were simple.

It took a moment for them to get into position, but Alexis and Caroline had trained with the hunters a few times, and while they weren't smooth yet, they understood each other. The humans didn't have any problem with Rowan and Alexis taking the lead of their group while Caroline watched their back. They might be hunters, but they weren't idiots, and they knew that the three of them were stronger than they could ever be.

They moved quietly and slowly as they walked into the grocery store. The air smelled dusty and made Alexis's nose itch, but he ignored it and focused on the job.

The nest.

Nesting Kudlaks were never good, and this time wasn't

any different. By the time the fight was over, Alexis was sweaty and bloody and standing over a bunch of dead bodies. He sucked in a breath, trying to calm his racing heart, while Rowan turned every Kudlak they'd killed so that he could see their faces. For some reason, he looked almost disappointed. Alexis didn't understand that.

"We killed many of them," he said. "It was a good night's work."

Rowan nodded, but he was distracted. "You and Caroline did a good job."

"You don't look like you believe that."

Rowan sighed and straightened from his crouch beside one of the bodies. "You really did a good job. I was just hoping we'd find a particular Kudlak."

That was new. "Who?"

Rowan hesitated. "I don't want to freak you out."

"I don't think anything can freak me out after what I saw during the wars and my many hunts."

Alexis was wrong about that because as Rowan told him about the Kudlak who'd tried to kill him because he'd killed his entire family like he was trying to collect them, his blood turned to ice.

Boyd couldn't stop thinking about what Clay had asked him earlier today. It had been a while since he'd thought about what he would have done if he hadn't become a hunter, and he didn't know how to deal with it. Talking about it with Clay had brought up everything he felt about hunting, even though he'd tried ignoring it since he'd moved into his new home. He wasn't sure he could for much longer. He realized that telling Clay and Rowan he didn't want to be a hunter would mean being kicked out of the clan, but could he really continue doing this?

He didn't want to, and he was scared that it would show when he fought. It would distract him and make him more vulnerable, and he didn't want to die because of that. He had too much to live for now that he had a home and Alexis.

Except he wouldn't have a home if he didn't continue being a hunter.

He groaned and kicked one of the trees he was standing next to. The tree didn't budge, but Boyd's foot hurt, and he glared at the trunk.

He was being an idiot. He should be in bed, trying to sleep so that he'd be rested tomorrow. Instead, he was walking around like an idiot, trying to make sense of his feelings and thoughts. Who would do that? It was a recipe for disaster, or at the very least, to be found by a Kudlak and skinned alive.

Boyd couldn't stop thinking about the future. Being here was part of it, but meeting Alexis had made it even more important. Boyd didn't want to lose his mate in any way, either by having to leave the village or by being killed by a Kudlak. Maybe he'd be allowed to stay if he and Alexis were together. Rowan and Clay weren't allowed to separate mates, and Boyd doubted they would even try to.

He hadn't thought of that solution before and didn't know why. It was probably because he and Alexis had just met, and he wasn't used to having a mate yet. After that first kiss, they'd only seen each other from afar, and it wasn't enough, but Boyd didn't want to push.

Maybe he should. Maybe Alexis would be his way into the village without being a hunter. Of course, Alexis would have to want to be with Boyd, but Boyd was pretty sure that wouldn't be a problem.

Or at least, he hoped it wouldn't be.

He wanted his mate to want him as much as he wanted him. He didn't think that was too much to ask, but he was still frightened. This felt like too many changes in too little time, and his mind spun at the thought of all of it. Not being a hunter would be another change, and he didn't know how he'd deal with it.

"I thought I heard a dumbass walking around the forest," Kendrick's voice said from behind Boyd, making him jump.

Boyd glared at his friend. "Are you following me?"

"Yeah. You have a stalker."

Boyd rolled his eyes. "You'd suck as a stalker."

"I don't know. You had no idea I was here until I spoke."

That much was true. Boyd hadn't heard his friend because he'd been too focused on his thoughts and trying to make sense of them.

"I don't think anyone should be in the forest this late at night. Let me walk you home," Kendrick said.

"I can find my way home on my own."

"I have no doubt you can, but it doesn't mean you should. Besides, I'm your neighbor. It's not like I'll be going far once I drop you at home."

Boyd nodded and turned to follow Kendrick. His friend kept peeking at him every so often, and eventually, Boyd had enough. "What?"

"I was just wondering how you've been doing. You never talk much, but you've been even quieter lately. Is it because we left the hunters?"

"I don't care about that. We did a good thing leaving Cornelius behind. I wasn't about to hurt children just because he thought it was right."

Kendrick nodded. "I'm with you on that. I only want to hurt people who deserve it, not kids. Hey, did you know that Devon is eighteen?"

Boyd blinked, trying to understand what Devon had to do with any of this. "I thought he was younger."

"Yeah, me, too. He looks way younger." Kendrick hesitated. "Don't tell anyone about this, all right?"

"What have you done?" Boyd asked with a groan.

"I haven't done anything."

"Doesn't sound like it."

Kendrick pushed Boyd but didn't put any strength in it, so Boyd didn't even stumble.

"Devon reminds me of my little brother. I miss my family and thought that maybe Devon and I could have that kind of relationship. We've been spending time together and everything, but a few days ago, he kissed me, or at least tried to."

Boyd made a strangled sound. "He's a kid."

"That's what I said when I pushed him away. He yelled at me that he just turned eighteen and that he was an adult, but it's not just his age. It's not even that he reminds me of my brother. Even though he's eighteen, he's just a kid, and I don't see him that way."

"Did you tell him all of that?"

Kendrick sighed. "He ran away before I could. He hasn't talked to me since then."

Boyd could see where both Kendrick and Devon were coming from. It couldn't be easy to be in Devon's position, and he was probably latching on to one of the people who was treating him right. If Boyd had to guess, he didn't think Devon actually had a thing for Kendrick. He just wanted to feel like people cared about him.

"But I don't really want to talk about it anymore because it's a mess. Why don't you tell me about the new guy?"

Boyd had a choice. He could act as if he didn't know what Kendrick was talking about, or he could be honest with him and tell him who Alexis was to him. He wasn't sure which solution was right, but he trusted Kendrick. "You can't tell anyone about this, either."

"Have the two of you been boning?"

"Can we not talk like frat boys? No, we haven't been sleeping together, but it's going to happen eventually."

"You're that confident?"

"I wouldn't be if he weren't my mate, but he is."

Kendrick stumbled on a root and almost fell on his face. Boyd caught him and kept him on his feet, but Kendrick pushed him away. "Asshole. Did you really have to tell me like that?"

"How did you want me to tell you?"

"Not when I'm walking in the dark in the middle of the forest." He faced Boyd. "You're really mates?"

"Yeah. It was a surprise to both of us, and we're still unsure where we stand, so I don't want you to tell anyone. We both have a lot of things to think through."

"But you're okay with it?"

Boyd didn't even have to think. "I am. I might not have a clue what I'm doing, but I'm his mate. That's all I need to know."

"Then I'm happy for you."

Boyd was happy, too. He hadn't allowed himself to think too hard about it before because he'd been terrified he would lose Alexis and the clan, but maybe he wouldn't have to. Maybe being with Alexis meant he could stay, even though he didn't want to be a hunter.

But first, he and Alexis needed to talk.

Boyd and Kendrick were silent as they walked home. They separated once they reached the houses, and Kendrick waved at Boyd before climbing his porch steps. Boyd turned to do the same, only to stop at the sight of someone sitting on the upper step.

"Who is it?" he called out.

The person got to their feet, and Boyd realized it was Alexis. He'd known that his mate was going on a hunt, so he was relieved that Alexis seemed all right. He'd clearly showered before coming here, but he was moving easily and like he hadn't been hurt.

His expression made Boyd rethink that.

"What happened?" he asked as he rushed toward his mate.

Whatever it was, whoever had hurt him, he'd find them and hurt them right back.

Boyd might not want to be a hunter anymore, but when it came to Alexis, he was ready to kill every single Kudlak in existence.

It hadn't been easy to listen to Rowan explain that a group of Kudlaks was playing a sick game with what remained of the Krsniks. He'd told Alexis that he was looking for a particular Kudlak who had told him that he wanted to finish his set— meaning that he'd killed the rest of Rowan's family and wanted to kill him, too, so he'd be able to boast about the fact that he'd destroyed an entire clan.

Alexis couldn't help but wonder if that was what had happened to his family. They'd been hunted and killed, and no one but him remained. It had been painful, but he hadn't thought it strange. Between Kudlak attacks and wars between the clans, many Krsniks had been killed.

But now he knew there was possibly something more to it, and he had no idea what to do with that knowledge. He wanted to hunt the Kudlak Rowan was after and torture answers out of him, but he doubted the Kudlak would give him anything.

At least Alexis didn't have anyone left. His clan was gone, and he was the only survivor. He wouldn't have to worry about anyone else dying.

Except that he did have to worry. He might not have any of his old clan members anymore, but he had a new clan. He had best friends and a mate, and they were all people the Kudlaks could take from him.

What would happen if they tried killing Jonas, Caroline, or

Boyd? Alexis would be destroyed even if the Kudlaks killed Rowan or Clay. He didn't know them well yet, but they'd welcomed him and his friends into the clan, and so far, they hadn't done anything that meant Alexis couldn't trust them. They were good people, and Alexis didn't want anything to happen to either of them.

"What happened?" Boyd gently pushed.

Alexis didn't want to talk about it yet. He would have to eventually, and way too soon, but right now, he wanted to forget what he knew. He wanted to focus on his mate and the future they had together.

If neither of them were killed.

He threw himself at Boyd. Boyd stumbled back, but he wrapped his arms around Alexis and kept both of them upright. Alexis grabbed Boyd's face and kissed him, and while Boyd made a startled sound, he kissed Alexis back as if this was normal for them. It wasn't yet, but eventually, it would be. They'd settle down as mates, find a way to make their lives work together and be happy.

Alexis wouldn't have it any other way, no matter who was out there wanting to kill him.

Boyd's back slammed against the front door. It was closed, so they didn't go any further. Alexis tried climbing his mate, and while Boyd did everything he could to keep them on their feet, there was a certain reluctance in his movements.

Alexis started to move back. "I'm sorry. I shouldn't use you to forget."

Boyd held him where he was. "You can use me for whatever you want or need. I'd like to know what's going on with you and why you're doing this, but you don't have to tell me if you don't feel comfortable with it."

"I feel comfortable with it. I'm just not ready. Besides, it's something that happened in the past."

"I want you to tell me about your past."

"I will."

Boyd stared at Alexis for a moment before nodding. "But not tonight."

It wasn't a question. He might not know what was going on in Alexis's mind, but he understood him.

Alexis made to kiss his mate again, but Boyd leaned away. He reached back without looking away from Alexis, and the front door opened.

Boyd smiled. "I have no problems with you using me, but not here where anyone can see us."

That was perfectly fine with Alexis. Actually, it was more than fine because he didn't want anyone to see Boyd. He was Alexis's mate and the only one who should see him like this.

As soon as the door was closed behind them, Alexis was on Boyd again. Boyd didn't seem to care. Alexis expected him to take him upstairs, but he carried Alexis into the living room instead. Thankfully, the couch was wide enough for both of them and when Boyd let himself fall backward, Alexis ended up on top of him. He tried to get off, but Boyd wouldn't let him go anywhere. He tightened his hold on Alexis and kissed a path down Alexis's neck. The only thing Alexis could do was tilt his head back to give his mate better access.

"I don't think this is the right moment for us to bond," Boyd murmured against the skin of Alexis's neck.

It took Alexis a moment to understand what Boyd was saying. "You thought I wanted to bond?"

"I'm trying not to be offended by the way you just said it," Boyd said with a snicker. "And no, I didn't think you were going to bite me. I just wanted you to know that while I do want to bond with you eventually, I don't think this is the right moment. You're obviously overwhelmed, and I don't want either of us to regret anything that happens tonight."

Alexis leaned back. "You'd regret bonding with me?"

"I'd regret bonding with you without thinking about it and

the consequences it would have."

Alexis understood where Boyd was coming from. He told himself not to be offended or sad at the thought that Boyd didn't want to bond with him because Boyd was right. Alexis was emotional right now, and while his entire being desperately wanted to claim Boyd and make him his, they'd just met and had plenty of time to get to know each other before that happened.

"I hadn't even thought about bonding with you tonight," Alexis confessed.

"Then we don't have to worry."

Alexis hoped he'd be able to control his instinct. Right now, it was telling him to bite his mate's neck, but that would be the worst thing he could do. So instead, he kissed Boyd again.

Boyd's hands landed on Alexis's ass. They slid upward, taking Alexis's sweater and t-shirt with them. Alexis sat up and grabbed both, taking them off in one movement that left Boyd staring at him with wide eyes. Alexis winked, realized it probably made him look like an asshole, and dove on top of his mate again.

The problem was that Boyd was still wearing his own sweater. Alexis had to help him get the garments off. When he threw them to the side, they landed on something that made a shattering glass sound when it fell to the floor.

They stared at each other with wide eyes. Alexis was almost afraid to check what they'd broken, but after a few seconds, Boyd shook his head and hooked a hand behind Alexis's neck again. "Don't care," he muttered.

Then he kissed Alexis.

It was easy to forget about the world and all the problems outside of this house when Alexis was in Boyd's arms. The need for Boyd consumed him, and even though they were touching as much as possible, it still wasn't enough. Alexis needed more.

He needed everything.

He pushed his hands between them to unfasten Boyd's jeans. They weren't as tight as his, so pushing them down Boyd's thighs was fairly easy. The same couldn't be said for his. He struggled once he had them undone, which for some reason, made Boyd laugh.

"I'm impatient, too, but I don't want you to hurt yourself," he said before gently helping Alexis to push his jeans down his ass.

Alexis didn't want to talk. The time for that was gone. Now was the time to focus on their bodies. He wanted Boyd to forget there was a world outside of this house. He wanted his mate to be entirely focused on him and nothing else.

He thought he got it when he wrapped his hand around both their cocks.

Boyd made a guttural sound and smashed their lips together with a bit too much force. Their teeth clacked together, but it was just for a few seconds. Boyd gentled the kiss, but his passion for Alexis was still very much present. Alexis could feel the ever-growing feelings that came from his mate in the way Boyd touched him as if he was precious and in the way they moved against each other.

He was in charge, and Boyd didn't seem to have a problem with that, but at the same time, Alexis felt like Boyd was the one in control. He'd stop what he was doing immediately if his mate told him this wasn't right for him.

He was glad Boyd didn't.

Alexis undulated his hips as he continued jacking them off. He needed more, but he didn't have the patience for it. As much as he wanted Boyd naked and to take his time exploring his body, it would have to wait. He needed to forget everything that wasn't them, and taking his time would give him too many opportunities to obsess over what he'd learned earlier. The way he and Boyd frantically moved together meant

Alexis couldn't focus on anything else, and he needed that.

His mate was the center of his universe, the only thing he wanted or needed to think about. The world would intrude in their cocoon soon enough. For now, it was okay to keep it outside.

"Faster," Boyd muttered against Alexis's lips.

Alexis obeyed. He wanted to give his mate everything. He wanted Boyd to lose his mind and want to do this again and again until they were both old and wrinkly. It felt like a lot, maybe even too much, but for the first time, Alexis wasn't afraid when he thought of the future. He knew he'd have one and that it would be happy.

Because Boyd would be in it.

Boyd grabbed Alexis's ass and pulled him even closer, smashing their bodies together. Alexis had to stop moving his hand, but that was okay because Boyd shuddered under him and spilled over their naked stomachs as Alexis gently bit his lower lip. The warmth of it and the way Boyd looked were enough to send Alexis over the edge, too. His instinct was to close his eyes as he came, but instead, he kept them wide open and stared at Boyd.

Boyd was staring back. His cheeks were flushed, his mouth slightly open, and his eyes wide with pleasure. Alexis felt so damn smug that he'd been the one to make him look that way, but he didn't feel that way for long because the emotions running through him were too much. He didn't close his eyes, but he leaned down and buried his face against Boyd's neck, placing a kiss in the very spot he yearned to bite.

Boyd shivered again, but he didn't let go of Alexis. They stayed in each other's arms as they allowed their bodies to come down from their hurried pleasure, and while Alexis knew they would have to talk soon, this was perfect for now.

Boyd was everything Alexis could ever have wanted and had never thought about. He'd taken Alexis by surprise, and while Alexis wasn't sure what their lives and future would be like, he was sure of one thing.

They'd deal with it together.

CHAPTER FIVE

Boyd rubbed his hands over his thighs. He couldn't believe he was about to do this.

When Alexis had suggested he be honest with Rowan and Clay, Boyd had panicked. Even though he knew Alexis was right and that the chances that his leaders would kick him out of the clan were small, it was still terrifying to think there was a possibility it would happen. Alexis had been trying to convince Boyd to talk to them for several days now, but Boyd had always brushed him off.

He hadn't been able to do so last night. Alexis had cornered him and told him that he wanted to be honest with everyone. He and his two best friends wanted to settle down and make the village their home, and he felt he couldn't do that if he wasn't honest with their leaders. He wasn't willing to hide that he and Boyd were together, and when Boyd had suggested they mention only the fact that they were mates, he'd seemed disappointed.

The last thing Boyd wanted to do was to disappoint his mate. He wanted to make Alexis happy and thought he was doing his best, but that wasn't true. He couldn't do his best when he couldn't give all of himself to his mate.

So here he was, standing in front of the door of the house where Rowan and Clay lived. The air smelled of fresh wood. Boyd knew they'd been renovating the inside. They hadn't wanted to take the house that was in better condition and had decided to leave it to Melissa, the Kudlak who'd taken Devon under her wing and had protected him along with her daughter. That was a sure sign that they were good leaders and probably that Boyd shouldn't be worried, but he felt the need to turn around and run away screaming.

A hand landed on the small of his back. He turned to Alexis, not knowing what to say but not surprised to see that his mate appeared worried.

"I can do this," Boyd promised.

"I never doubted that. If you don't feel ready, though, maybe you should wait. I don't want to push you into doing anything you're not ready for."

Boyd swallowed and glanced at the door again. "The problem is that I don't know if I'll ever be ready to do this. It's so much easier to hide."

"I don't know what to do. I want to push you because I truly believe you'll be happy once you do, but I feel guilty. You shouldn't be doing this just because of me."

Boyd didn't want Alexis to think he was responsible for any of this. He turned to his mate and dragged him into his arms, and like always, Alexis slotted against his chest like he belonged there. Even though he was the strongest physically, Boyd was bigger, and he felt like they were well-suited. They filled each other's holes — and not only physically.

"This has nothing to do with you," Boyd promised. "If it were only the mate thing, I'd be screaming it from the rooftops. I'm not ashamed of our relationship and want everyone to know about it. I wouldn't have told my best friends if I wanted to keep it a secret."

After telling Kendrick, Boyd had gone to Chris, too. He'd been a bit pissed that Boyd had gone to Kendrick first, but it didn't matter in the end. Boyd had been honest with them when it came to Alexis, and they were happy for him. They hadn't thought about the possibility that Boyd might not be a part of the clan, and Boyd had been trying to do the same.

He'd been spending time with Alexis, fixing his yard and

the house, and training. One of those things made him want to puke, while the others made him happy. The problem was that he didn't know what he could do for the village if he wasn't a hunter. He needed to find something that would be useful to everyone and would allow him to earn enough money to survive since if he quit being a hunter, the council wouldn't be paying him anymore. All of that was scary enough that it made his mouth dry at the thought of doing something about it.

"Let's go home," Alexis murmured.

Boyd shook his head, grabbed his mate's hand, and knocked on the door before he could think better of it. His hand shook, but he ignored it and clung to Alexis.

The door opened after only a few seconds. Clay stood there, smiling like an idiot as he stared at Boyd and Alexis's hands. "Finally. I was worried you'd spend the rest of the night on the porch."

"Don't be an asshole," Rowan called out from somewhere in the house. "Let them in."

Clearly, they both thought that Boyd and Alexis were here to tell them they were together. They weren't wrong, but that was only part of the reason for their presence. It was a part they'd be happy about, but what about the other one?

Boyd had taken this step, and he needed to see it through. It was what Alexis wanted, but more importantly, what Boyd needed. He'd had enough of being a hunter, putting himself in danger, and killing people. He didn't even care that they deserved it. It had become too much for him, and he didn't think he could go on a hunt without screaming.

They followed Clay into the house. Like Boyd had suspected, there were signs that the place was being worked on. The banister of the staircase that led upstairs was new, which explained the smell of fresh wood. Someone was painting the walls in the entrance, and the furniture in the living room was covered with plastic.

Clay led the way to the kitchen. That room looked like they were done with it, and Rowan was at the stove cooking. Boyd's stomach twisted, and he wondered if Rowan and Clay would be offended if he threw up on their kitchen island.

Rowan looked back at them and put down the wooden spoon he'd been using. "Please don't listen to Clay. He's an idiot."

Clay grinned and snatched Rowan around the waist, pulling him closer. "Maybe, but I'm an idiot you love."

They were relaxed, and Boyd wondered if he was about to ruin their evening. Hell, he wondered if he was about to ruin his life.

"Are you here to tell us that you're together?" Clay asked, nodding at Boyd's hand that was still linked with Alexis's.

Alexis looked at Boyd. He would let him do this on his own, which was understandable but terrifying. Boyd didn't know where to start, but he decided to go with the easiest thing to admit. "We are. Alexis told me I'm his mate, and we've decided to give it a try."

Clay's smile widened. "I suspected that something like that was happening, but Rowan told me to keep my nose where it belonged. Congrats, guys." He looked at Alexis and winked. "And welcome to the family."

They were accepting this so easily, and clearly, they'd been expecting it. Boyd wondered if they were expecting what he was about to say next, too.

"There's something else."

Rowan moved closer to Boyd. "Are you finally ready to admit you don't want to be a hunter anymore?" he asked gently.

Boyd gaped at him. "How did you know?"

"It's kind of obvious. Don't get me wrong, you're trying hard to train and be there for the others, but you're also reluctant. I don't think you want to be sent on hunts anymore, and

I've never seen you happier than when you're working on your home and yard."

He and Clay looked at each other. It was as if they were talking without using words, and Boyd could only stand there and wait for them to be done.

Thankfully, it was only a few seconds before Rowan turned to him again. "Clay and I should have been clearer. Krsnik families are usually made up of hunters, but their villages and clans aren't. There are many people needed to have a successful clan, and most of them are there for support. They take care of the village, deal with the everyday jobs, and things like that. They're store owners, family members, school teachers, and everyone else. I don't expect you to remain a hunter if you don't feel up for it. You can be whatever you want, Boyd."

It was more than Boyd had expected, and he didn't know how to answer Rowan's unspoken question.

What did he want to be?

Alexis was happy for Boyd. He hadn't expected Rowan and Clay to kick Boyd out just because he didn't want to be a hunter, but Boyd had believed they might, and it was good that he could finally get over it. These people would allow him to be whatever he wanted, even if that wasn't being a hunter.

"I don't know what to say," Boyd murmured. "Thank you."

"I never expected to be a clan leader, but I remember how it was when I grew up. I want to be the same kind of leader as my grandfather and father were. I want my people to be happy, and if hunting doesn't make you happy, then please, don't force it."

"You need more hunters, though."

Alexis wanted to ask Boyd why he was doing this. He'd gotten what he wanted. He wouldn't be forced to be a hunter. Why was he arguing with Rowan?

"I think we'll always need more hunters. It doesn't mean I'm going to force anyone into this life. You've been through a lot, and you've been a hunter for years. Maybe this is the right time for you to settle down and allow yourself to rest."

"But you have to promise to tell me if you need help. I can continue training, just in case, and if you ever need more people, I can help."

Alexis could tell Boyd was still afraid he was going to get kicked out. It was ridiculous, but it was a fear his mate would need to get over in time. He'd only just found the clan and a new home. It made sense that his main fear was to lose them.

"We can do that," Rowan said with a smile. "Now, how about the two of you have dinner with us?"

Alexis wanted nothing more than to drag Boyd home and have his way with him, but he thought Boyd needed this. The more time he spent with his leaders, the more he could see that they meant what they were saying.

A phone started ringing. Rowan groaned, then raised a finger to tell them to wait. He grabbed his phone from the kitchen island and answered. "Rowan Harper here."

His expression was serious as he listened. Alexis could hear someone talking on the other side, but he couldn't make sense of the words because he wasn't close enough. From Rowan's expression, it was clear that whatever was happening wasn't good.

"We'll be there right away," Rowan said, confirming Alexis's fears.

Rowan hung up. "The council got the news that a family of Vila headed our way was attacked."

"Let's go save them," Clay said as he got his phone out.

A few seconds later, Alexis's phone vibrated in his pocket.

He knew Clay had to have sent a group text to every hunter, so he didn't bother to check the phone.

He never went anywhere without his weapons, which meant he was ready to go whenever Rowan and Clay were ready. They had to wait for the other hunters, and in the meantime, they got ready to go. Alexis borrowed a few more weapons, hiding them on his body. He could already feel the adrenaline, and he sucked in a breath and told himself to calm down.

"Do we know how many Kudlaks are attacking?" Boyd asked.

Alexis didn't like that he'd grabbed weapons, too. Rowan and Clay had just told him that he didn't need to be a hunter, yet he was clearly going with them. Alexis wanted to tell him to stay back, but he wouldn't. Boyd could make his own decisions, and if he wanted to come, then he should. This would probably be his last hunt, and Alexis had no idea how either of them would deal with hunting together.

They were about to find out.

"The council only had a few details," Rowan explained. "It's more than one, though."

"How did they find out?"

"One of the Vila managed to call their emergency number. They couldn't stay on the line for long, which means we won't know what's going on exactly until we get there." Rowan walked out the front door. "We need to hurry."

Thankfully, everyone else was already gathered in front of the house, including Nysys. Alexis had no idea why he was always the one shimmering them back and forth, but it was none of his business. As long as the guy didn't get hurt and was able to shimmer them back, he didn't care why he was here.

There was no banter this time. Everyone grabbed Nysys where they could, and he shimmered them right away. Alexis didn't know how shimmering worked in detail, so he had no idea how Nysys managed to find the family being attacked. He suspected it had to do with Rowan, who'd closed his eyes as they left. Maybe Alexis should ask once they were home.

They moved as soon as it was safe to let go of Nysys. Alexis took a second to look around and take in the situation. He didn't like going in without knowing what was happening, but he understood that sometimes, getting any more details than what the council had already told them was impossible.

They'd landed in an empty field. A small group of people was scattered close by, their backs pressed together as they faced the Kudlaks attacking them. The field was empty except for them, and it was freezing cold. That didn't stop the Kudlaks from doing what they did best.

Terrorizing innocent people.

As Alexis watched, a Kudlak with long brown hair snapped forward. She was reaching for a child hidden in the group of Vila, but a man with short blond hair slapped his hand on her arm. Sparks shot up, and she jerked back. The air smelled of burning flesh, making Alexis's stomach turn.

"What was that?" Boyd asked.

"Vila are a kind of fairy. They use magic, which is what you saw." Alexis looked at his mate. "Ready?"

Boyd nodded. His expression was fierce, and Alexis didn't want to doubt him. He had to trust that Boyd knew what he was doing and that he wouldn't push himself to do something he couldn't do or wasn't ready for. Boyd was here, which meant he'd be fighting, and Alexis couldn't afford to obsess over him.

The others were already moving forward, but Alexis grabbed Boyd's sweater and pulled him forward. He smashed their lips together, telling himself that this wasn't their last kiss.

It couldn't be.

"Be careful," he ordered as he let go of Boyd.

His mate grinned. "Same goes for you. Whoever kills the most Kudlaks wins, all right?"

Alexis snorted. There was no way Boyd would win, but Alexis suspected that winning wasn't the reason Boyd was doing this. He wanted Alexis to be focused on the fight and do his best, which was what Alexis was going to do.

He'd counted five Kudlaks, which was unusual. Usually, they hunted alone or in couples. Even when they nested, only two or three adults were in the nest. Seeing five of them working together made Alexis wonder what they were up to.

"You," Alexis heard Rowan yell.

Rowan was a calm fighter. He kept his head in the game and focused on what he was doing. Tonight was different. Alexis had no idea what was happening, but Rowan threw himself at one of the Kudlaks. He moved jerkily, and he wasn't focused.

That wasn't good.

There was nothing Alexis could do for him. Besides, Clay had his mate's back. He was already jumping on the Kudlak, trying to distract him from Rowan, who was trying to stab him.

The Kudlak laughed and flung Clay aside.

"It looks like I'll have another opportunity to finish my Harper clan set," he said, gloating.

That was when Alexis understood who the Kudlak was. His stomach churned, knowing that he'd killed most of Rowan's family. Rowan wanted revenge, which was why he was reacting the way he was.

Alexis needed to trust his leaders and have faith that they knew what to do, even though it didn't look like it. In the meantime, he had another four Kudlaks to deal with.

The hunters had divided into groups of three or four, each taking on a different Kudlak. It was the only way for human hunters to do this and not be killed. Boyd was working with Chris, Kendrick, and Rachel, and since Caroline was busy with one of the other groups, Alexis decided to go help them. He could keep an eye on Boyd while giving him the space he needed to do this.

Boyd wasn't just a guy. Even though he didn't want to be a hunter, he'd trained and hunted Kudlaks for years.

Alexis needed to believe he could win this fight.

As soon as Alexis stepped into the fight, Boyd knew he no longer had to worry. He, Chris, Kendrick, and Rachel had been holding their own, but it was never easy to kill a Kudlak. They were fast and strong, and they could shift into animals.

Which was what the man they were fighting did. As Boyd stumbled backward, the Kudlak shifted into a black lion. He roared, sending a shiver down Boyd's spine. It wasn't the first time he had to fight a shifted Kudlak, but it never got any less terrifying.

But Boyd and the hunters weren't hunting alone anymore. He noticed Alexis grin just before his body started changing, too. His clothes stretched around him, and Boyd realized that his and Caroline's clothing was made for this. It didn't tear as Alexis's body became the body of a white panther.

He was magnificent. Even though it was dark, the moon was high in the sky, and with nothing in the way, Boyd could easily see his mate. He'd always thought Alexis was graceful when he moved, and now, he understood why. His shifter form was as graceful as his human one and just as beautiful.

A hand grabbed Boyd's elbow. He turned, ready to attack, but it was Kendrick. Now that the Kudlak and Alexis had shifted, it would be harder for them to help fight. Attacking a lion face-on was way too dangerous, but that didn't mean they had to stand by and watch what was happening. Boyd didn't think he could do that. Even though he knew Alexis had been born to do this and had been hunting for decades, it was too easy to imagine the lion tearing him to pieces.

"Go to the Vila," Kendrick said. "Focus on them. We'll help Alexis."

Boyd was tempted to tell Kendrick to fuck off. The only reason he didn't was that Kendrick wasn't pushing him to do it because he thought he was too weak or incapable of defending himself. He was giving him an out of having to watch his mate fight the Kudlak, and Boyd was grateful for that.

He nodded and put one of his knives back into its sheath. He kept the other in his hand, just in case, but all the Kudlaks who'd been attacking were busy. As Boyd watched, Caroline jumped onto the back of one of the biggest Kudlaks Boyd had ever seen. She wrapped her arms around the man's neck, and Boyd had to look away when blood spurted.

He was used to blood and gore, but he understood where Jonas was coming from when he loudly declared this wasn't a life for him. Boyd didn't want it to be his life. He didn't want to have to kill anymore.

Thankfully, it looked like he wouldn't have to.

He left the others to their job and rushed toward the Vila family. He counted a dozen people, from elderly to children. The adults had gathered around the elders and the kids, protecting them from the Kudlaks. They appeared both relieved and wary when Boyd reached them. Nysys was with them, and Boyd was grateful he'd kept them calm.

"My name is Boyd," he said, hoping to reassure them. "I'm a member of the new Harper clan."

The adults looked at each other, and Boyd wondered what they thought. He and Alexis had been talking about what the Krsnik clans had been like before, so he knew that Krsnik never lived alone in their villages. The Vila who lived with them taught them magic and protected their homes, and he couldn't help but wonder who these Vila were and what they were doing here. They weren't far from the village, but Boyd didn't want to assume that was where they'd been headed, even though they desperately needed more clan members.

Nysys had reached them before Boyd, and he was talking to one of the elderly women. Boyd focused his attention on the people standing right in front of him, trying to understand who he should talk to.

"Is everyone all right?" he asked.

A man stepped forward. There was no way to know how old he was since he was a supernatural creature, but he appeared to be in his late twenties. His long blond hair was braided and hung over his shoulder, and there was a streak of dirt on his cheek. He kept his distance from Boyd, but he didn't seem afraid.

"Dermot is wounded," he said. "And the kids are scared, but they're fine. I don't think they can continue walking. Esta fell, and while she says she's all right, I don't want her to continue walking, either."

"They won't have to," Nysys said. "I can shimmer all of you back to the village."

The man looked at Boyd for confirmation. Boyd had no idea why except that maybe it was because he was clearly a hunter.

"Nysys is part of our family," he said. "You can trust him."

"I don't think we have any choice. I'm Tomlin."

Boyd nodded. They'd have time for introductions once everyone was safe.

He stayed with the family until they were ready for Nysys to shimmer them away. He and Nysys exchanged a glance, and Nysys nodded. "I'll be right back. I can bring reinforcements if you want."

Boyd looked back at the fight. Two of the Kudlaks had been killed, and one was trying to run away, but the other two were still fighting. He didn't know if they would need help, but it wouldn't be a bad thing to have backup, just in case.

"You know where to find us," he said.

Nysys shimmered everyone away. Now that they were gone, Boyd didn't have to focus on them anymore. He didn't think he could fight with Alexis, but that didn't mean he couldn't fight at all.

Rowan was still fighting the Kudlak he'd jumped when they'd arrived. Clay was there, too, but even though there were two of them, the Kudlak was moving as if he was taking a stroll in the park rather than fighting two hunters.

Boyd headed that way. It was probably a stupid idea, but he wasn't about to stand in the middle of the field and watch the people he cared about be hurt when he could do something about it.

"You don't have to do this," Rowan said when Boyd reached him.

He was panting, and there was a cut on his cheek. He seemed to be all right beyond that, so Boyd didn't worry too much.

"I wouldn't be here if I didn't want to do it," Boyd told him.

Rowan nodded and threw himself at the Kudlak again. Clay did the same, and Boyd joined in. He'd get in a few hits while the Kudlak was distracted by Clay and Rowan.

Hunting was hard, and tonight wasn't any different. Eventually, Boyd had to take a step back. He was out of breath, and his entire body hurt because the Kudlak had slammed him against the ground too many times. It was a miracle he hadn't torn off Boyd's head yet.

A loud yell made Boyd jump. he turned, and he was running before he could think about what was happening. He wasn't entirely sure what he was seeing, but Alexis was back in his human form and in the arms of one of the remaining Kudlaks. The man had buried his face against Alexis's neck, and while Alexis was trying to push him away, the Kudlak wasn't budging. Kendrick was pulling on him from behind, but it was as if the Kudlak couldn't even feel him.

He was drinking Alexis's blood.

A shiver of horror ran down Boyd's body, but he told himself to ignore it. He raised his knives and screamed, and thankfully, Kendrick understood what was happening before Boyd reached them. He jumped off the Kudlak's back, and Boyd slammed both of his knives into the man.

That was enough to make him let go. He roared at the sky, but Boyd didn't wait for his reaction. He pulled the knives out and moved around the Kudlak, pushing him away from Alexis.

Boyd's mate had fallen to his knees. He was clutching his neck, and even though it was dark, Boyd could see the blood streaming from the wound. Could Krsniks die from blood loss? Boyd had no idea and no intention of finding out.

He crouched into a defensive position. Whatever the Kudlak threw at him, he'd defend Alexis.

Alexis attempted to get to his feet, but his neck burned, and he could feel blood streaming from the wound. He needed to protect Boyd. He needed to make sure the Kudlak didn't kill his mate.

Two hands grabbed his shoulders and pushed him back down. He snarled at the person only to realize it was Kendrick.

"You're not going to be any good in this fight," Kendrick told him. "Stay where you are."

"I need to help Boyd."

"You don't. He's not fighting alone."

Alexis turned. He shouldn't have been surprised to see Caroline had joined Boyd, and she wasn't the only one. Chris and Rachel were helping them, and between the four of them, they were pushing the Kudlak back. Alexis was sure it also had something to do with the stab wounds in the Kudlak's back.

Alexis's mate was fierce, and he'd saved Alexis. Someone else would have stepped in if he hadn't, but even though Boyd hated all of this, it didn't seem to matter right now. He was fighting as hard as he could to save Alexis.

Kendrick ran toward the fight. He got Boyd's attention, and when they nodded at each other, Alexis knew Boyd would be all right. He breathed easier when his mate stepped away from the fight and rushed toward him. The Kudlak was slowing down, anyway, and as Alexis watched, Caroline stabbed him in the heart.

Then Alexis couldn't see anything but Boyd.

His mate knelt in front of him, dropping his knives as if they didn't matter. He reached for Alexis, but he didn't touch him. Instead, he kept his hands hovering between them, almost as if he was afraid Alexis would break.

"What happened?" Boyd asked.

His voice was rough with emotion. The sound made Alexis want to cry, but he cleared his throat and tried to gather himself.

Dammit. Even clearing his throat hurt. "He attacked Chris. I did what I had to do and stepped between them. I can take a bite, but a human would have died."

Boyd gently touched Alexis's hand that was clasped on the wound. "I don't know if you can take this kind of wound, either. It's bleeding a lot." He swallowed heavily. "What can I do? How do I make you better?"

"He needs blood," Rowan said.

He'd been fighting with the Kudlak who'd killed his family, but there were no signs of the asshole anymore. Rowan was holding one of his arms against his chest while Clay was limping, but they were breathing and moving, which meant they'd be all right.

"What kind of blood? Where do we get it?" Boyd asked.

"Human blood. It's the easiest and fastest way for him to heal."

"I'm human."

Alexis almost laughed. "I can't take your blood," he told Boyd.

Boyd looked offended. Alexis needed to explain himself before he fainted. The world was already going darker around the edges, which didn't bode well.

"Why not? Is there something wrong with my blood?"

"There's nothing wrong with any part of you, but you're my mate. If I were to bite you and drink your blood, it would start the bond between us."

Boyd looked at Alexis like he was an idiot. "That's your problem? I don't care. I want us to bond."

"It's too soon."

"Well, it's not going to happen at all if you die, so you'd better take my blood, you asshole. I don't care how much you have to take. I need you to survive this." He looked up at Rowan. "How do I do it?"

Alexis doubted that anything he could say would change his mate's mind. If he was honest, he was glad that Boyd was offering. He'd drunk blood from countless humans before, but never again. He hadn't drunk from anyone since he'd met Boyd, and his mate would be the only human he'd ever take blood from for the rest of his life. He wished it wasn't happening in these circumstances, but he was eager to taste Boyd.

Alexis didn't think he'd ever have enough of his mate.

"It's better if he takes from the neck," Rowan explained. "There are other arteries, but I don't think you want to take your pants off here. Clay and I will help keep him in a comfortable position."

Boyd nodded and sat on the cold ground. He hesitated for a moment, and Alexis realized why when his mate gently grabbed him. He was bigger than Alexis, so it was easy to manhandle him into the right position in his lap.

Apparently, the right position was Alexis facing him and wrapping his legs around his waist.

It looked like they were having sex.

Alexis could feel the heat of Boyd's skin and knew his mate was blushing. He grinned, even though it felt like his entire body hurt, including his face and his lips. "I didn't know you were into this kind of thing," he slurred.

"Usually, I'm not. I can't think of anything worse than having someone watch us having sex." Boyd's hand gently cradled the back of Alexis's neck. "But we're not having sex. I'm saving your life, so you better start drinking."

He didn't have to ask twice. Alexis could feel it wouldn't be long before he was unconscious, and if that happened, he wouldn't be able to drink.

So when Boyd guided his face toward the crook of his neck, he went for it.

The scent of his mate was delicious. Even though Boyd smelled like blood, sweat, and earth, Alexis couldn't think of anything better. He nuzzled his mate's skin, smiling again when Boyd groaned.

Then he struck.

Alexis had done this thousands of times. He knew exactly where to bite and how to make it so that it didn't hurt. It was even more important now that he was doing it with his mate, and he was careful as he started drinking. He needed to take enough so that he'd heal, but not too much. He had to keep his cool and remember who he was biting.

It was impossible to forget it. Boyd was all around him and inside of him. He was Alexis's future, his everything. Alexis would never do anything that would hurt him.

Boyd's arms curled around Alexis, keeping him in place. Alexis tightened his legs around his mate's waist, almost letting go of the wound when he felt Boyd's cock twitch between them. He was getting hard, too, which meant it would be uncomfortable and awkward once this was over.

He didn't care. He wouldn't have it any other way.

Well, he wished they were doing this in bed naked and not because he was wounded, but that was okay.

The next time he drank from his mate, they'd do it the other way.

Alexis felt the moment his side of the bond settled into place. It was confusing because it wasn't complete, but he'd never ask Boyd to finish it, especially not in these circumstances. They needed to talk first, and thanks to Boyd, Alexis would have the opportunity to do so.

He leaned back, but Boyd didn't let him go. Alexis licked the wound on his mate's neck, probably for longer than he should. Boyd wasn't bleeding anymore, but he still tasted of copper and sweat, and Alexis loved it.

Someone cleared their throat behind them. "Not that I'm not happy you're alive, but we have things to do," Clay said.

Alexis glared at him, but the human was grinning.

"That was interesting," he said.

"You're never going to let me forget about this, are you?" Boyd asked.

Clay leaned down to pat his shoulder. "You know me better than that. Besides, you're like me now. We're both Krsniks sippy cups."

"It doesn't mean I want to talk about what happened."

Clay whistled as he walked away. Alexis still felt weak, but that was normal. He'd feel better soon, and while he wanted nothing more than to stay where he was, he couldn't.

"Come on. Let's go see what the outcome of this fight was.".

Once they had, he'd drag Boyd home and into bed and re-fuse to leave for the next twelve hours.

At least.

CHAPTER SIX

B oyd helped Alexis to his feet. "Are you sure you're all right? You should stay here, and I'll go see what's going on."

"I promise I'm fine."

Alexis sounded fine, but Boyd was still freaking out. He couldn't believe how close he'd come to losing his mate, and he wasn't sure what he'd do when Alexis went on the next hunt on his own.

He rubbed his face. He couldn't think like that. He was sure Alexis had been wounded many times over the decades, yet he was still here. He was fine, and that wasn't going to change just because Boyd wasn't there to provide him with blood.

Alexis was lucky Boyd had been there, but if he hadn't been, Boyd had no doubt that Kendrick, Chris, or even one of the other hunters would have offered their blood. None of them wanted Alexis to die. Boyd's best friends definitely didn't.

Boyd noticed that Nysys was back. He stood with a blond man Boyd was pretty sure he'd noticed in the group earlier, but he had no idea why Nysys would bring him back.

"What's going on?" he asked as he wrapped an arm around his mate's waist and helped him walk toward them.

Nysys gestured at the man. "This is Tristan. He's half Nix and offered to help me heal the wounded."

"Can I take a look at your neck?" Tristan asked Alexis.

"You can, but I'm fine."

Boyd would feel better if a healer checked him over, so he

stayed where he was and kept Alexis in place. He saw Alexis roll his eyes, but thankfully, his mate didn't argue. He allowed Tristan to place his hand on his neck, and Boyd stared as a soft glow emanated from it.

"You lost a lot of blood, but you've already started to replenish it," Tristan said as he stepped back. "You'll be fine."

"Told you so. You should check the others, especially the humans."

Tristan nodded and went to work with Nysys. Even though Boyd knew Alexis was fine, he wasn't about to let him go, so he guided him toward Rowan and Clay. They stood with Rachel and Caroline while the other hunters gathered the dead bodies. Luckily, no one from the Vila family had been killed. The bodies belonged to the Kudlaks, who had attacked them.

"I've heard of him," Caroline was saying. "I'd never seen him before, though."

Rowan didn't look happy. "We have to find more information about him."

"We have to find more information about the people he works with, too," Clay said. "I still can't believe there's a group of Kudlaks hunting specific Krsnik clans."

From what Boyd had seen over the years, he could easily believe they could be so cruel. He wasn't surprised that Kudlaks were vindictive assholes, and it would make sense that at least some of them would want to get revenge for the Kudlaks the clans had killed.

"That was the Kudlak you told me about?" Alexis asked when they reached the little group.

Rowan nodded. "I still don't know who he is. Did you recognize him?"

"No. I don't like this, though. If this Kudlak and who knows how many others are hunting clans, they might come for us."

Boyd's stomach churned. He didn't think he could stand going on another hunt with his mate. He'd be worried if he had to wait at home for Alexis to return, but it would still be better than watching Alexis being hurt. He trusted his mate to come back to him alive and in one piece, but he didn't trust himself not to freak out if they did this together.

Nothing about it was going to be easy. Boyd had to choose the less difficult option, and for him, it was to stay at home and find another job. He didn't think Alexis would want him on his next hunt, either. It had to have been as terrifying for him as it had been for Boyd, especially because Boyd was human. It would have been easy for one of the Kudlaks to kill him.

"I hate being a hunter," he blurted out.

Everyone turned to look at him.

"Please tell us how you feel," Rachel teased.

Boyd swallowed. "I'm sorry. I didn't mean to blurt it out, but after tonight, I'm convinced more than ever that my place is in the village. I can't do this again."

Rowan nodded. "I don't expect you to continue doing it. I didn't expect you to come today, either. We would have been fine without you."

But Alexis wouldn't have been, so Boyd couldn't regret it. He just knew that it would be his last hunt.

He breathed a sigh of relief. He'd never have to do this ever again. He was free of the hunt, even though he would never be free of Kudlaks. He wouldn't have to deal with them anymore, though, and a weight lifted from his shoulders. He'd been so freaking worried about what would happen if he decided he didn't want to be a hunter anymore, but now that all of this happened, he realized how stupid he'd been. Rowan and Clay wouldn't kick him out. Alexis wouldn't want him any less. They knew him and liked him for who he was, even though he wasn't a hunter.

"I'm sorry to lose a hunter, but I'm sure we'll find more," Rowan continued. "Considering what we know now, I'm going to contact the council. They need to be aware of the fact that a group of Kudlaks is hunting clans and organizing. They've never done that before, and there's no way to know the end result. The council can help us find more hunters. Maybe they can even send a few enforcers to keep the village safe."

That was all Boyd wanted. A place to call home, a family, and to be safe. Unfortunately, no one would be safe until the Kudlaks were gone, which would be almost impossible to achieve, but they'd never stop fighting.

Well, Boyd would, but others would take his place. He wouldn't be doing this if he wasn't sure Rowan and Clay had everything in hand.

"How about we go home?" Rowan asked, raising his voice. "I called the council, and they're sending a team of enforcers to take care of the bodies."

"Really?" Alexis asked. "Maybe I should've worked for them sooner. I've always taken care of my bodies on my own."

Caroline snorted. "You left them where you killed them. That's not taking care of them."

"Details."

Boyd grinned and buried his face against Alexis's hair. He didn't know what the future held for them, but he did know that Alexis would be by his side. That was all he cared about.

He looked around as the others gathered around them. Since there was another Nix, they split into two groups, and of course Boyd stuck by Alexis's side. He clasped Tristan's shoulder, and he'd never been happier to see the village.

The people surrounding him were his family. He might not be going out to fight with them anymore, but he could do other things to make their lives easier. He wasn't sure what he wanted to do in the village yet, but he'd find out.

"How is your family?" Rowan asked Tristan.

"Nysys and I healed them before coming back. They're fine but scared and don't know where to go."

"I want to talk to all of you, but that can wait until tomorrow. We have plenty of empty houses. Not all of them are in good condition, but you can choose any you want and settle down there for the night. We'll talk again tomorrow and decide what's next."

Tristan looked overwhelmed, so it wasn't a surprise when he allowed Clay to guide him away. Tristan's family was huddled together, but they rushed toward him as soon as he stepped away from the group.

Boyd wanted nothing more than to drag Alexis home, but he couldn't forget about Alexis's family. They needed to reassure Jonas that everything was all right and that Alexis and Caroline were fine.

But once that was done, there would be no stopping Boyd from taking care of his mate.

"Alexis!"

Alexis almost groaned at the sound of Jonas's voice. He loved his friend, but right now, he wanted nothing more than to go home, shower, and go to bed. He wanted to take care of his mate and to make sure Boyd ate and drank enough to replenish the blood he'd given him, and he wanted to hold him as they slept. Was that too much to ask?

Jonas appeared in the middle of the small group of people huddled to the side. He rushed forward, ignoring everyone but Alexis. Seeing him and how worried he looked made Alexis feel guilty. Yes, he wanted to go home, but he could take the time to reassure his best friend that he was all right.

He opened his arms, and Jonas slammed against him. They

stumbled back, but thankfully, Boyd was there. He wrapped an arm around Alexis's shoulders, holding him in place. When Alexis looked up at him, he didn't appear angry. He was smiling as if he understood what was happening.

He probably did. He and his best friends had been hunters for years. They had to have gone through similar situations, so they understood where Jonas was coming from.

Jonas grabbed both of Alexis's shoulders and pushed him back to look at him. "What happened? I asked those people when they got here, but they couldn't tell me anything. Then I see you, and you're all dirty with blood, including your neck." He gently poked at the wound in Alexis's neck. Alexis winced and grabbed Jonas's hand, squeezing it. "I'm fine."

"That doesn't look like you're fine."

"I'll *be* fine, then." The wound was sore, but it was healed. Thanks to the blood Boyd had given Alexis and Tristan's healing, Alexis would be as good as new by tomorrow morning. "Boyd and Tristan took care of me after I was bitten."

Jonas's gaze jerked to Boyd. "What did you do?"

"He gave me his blood," Alexis said before Boyd could open his mouth. "And yes, we both know what it means. He did it to save my life, and I'm grateful."

Jonas turned and threw himself into Boyd's arms. Boyd's eyes went wide, and he awkwardly wrapped his arms around Jonas as if he was afraid to break him. Alexis almost laughed. It was good to see them together. He wanted his mate and his best friend to get along and be close.

"Thank you," Jonas said. "I don't know what I'd do if anything happened to Alexis or Caroline. Die, probably."

Boyd patted Jonas's back. "You'd be all right even if something happened to them. You're not alone anymore, remember?"

Jonas was crying when he stepped back. Alexis wanted to comfort him and make sure he was all right, but he wanted to do the same with Boyd and was torn. Thankfully, Caroline wasn't far, and Jonas threw himself at her as soon as she appeared by Alexis's side. That allowed Alexis to lean against Boyd, and he wondered how long it would be before they were allowed to go home. He needed a nap, dammit.

He turned his attention to the family they'd saved from the Kudlaks. Rowan was quietly talking to one of them, and since Alexis was curious and knew he wouldn't be going to bed anytime soon, he grabbed his mate's hand and dragged him closer.

"You don't have to explain anything tonight," Rowan was saying.

"We might not have to, but I wouldn't want you to believe we led the Kudlaks to you. I want to explain what happened and why we're here."

Alexis looked the Vila up and down. He was used to dealing with them since the village where he'd lived before had plenty of them. It had been a long time since he'd seen one, though, and he'd often wondered if they were gone like the clans.

"Hey, Tomlin," Boyd said when they reached the group.

Alexis blinked up at him. "You know him?"

"We talked just a few seconds during the fight," Boyd answered before turning his attention to Tomlin. "No one here thinks you led the Kudlaks to our village. You don't have to worry about that."

Tomlin straightened his back. "That's good, but I still want to talk to your leader."

"Then I'm listening," Rowan said.

Tomlin looked back at the rest of his family. A few nodded at him, which was probably what he was waiting for because he was ready when he turned back to Rowan.

"We heard about this village through the grapevine. Is it true that you're planning on making it a real Krsnik village?"

"That's the goal," Rowan confirmed. "I realize it will take a while, but eventually, I want this place to be like the places where we used to live when the clans were still alive."

Tomlin nodded. "That's why we're here. Every Krsnik clan needs Vila."

"You don't have to explain that to me. I'm well aware of it."

"Then we'd like to request to officially become part of your clan. I realize you probably want some time to talk to each and every one of us, but it's why we're here. We want to help you fight the Kudlaks, as well as protect your village and teach you magic. We want to go back to the traditions we shared before the Kudlaks destroyed everything."

Alexis pressed his lips together. He'd never thought this would happen. After he lost his clan and all the clans had been destroyed, he'd thought that was it. There had been no way for him to imagine they would eventually do this. Rowan was putting a clan together. He was giving all of them a new place to call home and a family, and Alexis didn't know how he could ever thank him enough.

"We'd be happy to welcome all of you," Rowan said with a smile. "Not all traditions should stay traditions, but this one, I'll be more than happy to keep. We need you."

Tomlin nodded. "There aren't many of you."

"Not yet, but our numbers are growing. Alexis, Jonas, and Caroline recently joined us, and I'm sure other Krsniks will come once they find out about this place."

"Alexis?" a voice asked from the back of the group.

Alexis watched as the group parted to let through an older Vila. It took him a moment, but when he recognized him, his eyes widened, and he stumbled forward. "Gary?"

The Vila came to a stop in front of Alexis. Alexis was sure it *was* Gary, who'd lived with his clan before it was destroyed. He'd thought everyone else had died, but he'd been wrong because Gary was standing in front of him. He looked the same, albeit older, and it was a blast from the past that Alexis didn't know how to deal with.

His throat tightened, and his eyes burned, and he stared at the man in front of him, trying to make sense of what he was seeing.

"I thought you were dead," Gary said.

Alexis chuckled. "Same. I thought everyone was dead."

Gary shrugged one shoulder. "I would have been if these guys hadn't taken me in. They made me part of their family."

"That's good."

Alexis and Gary hadn't been close, but Alexis couldn't stop himself from grabbing him and pulling him into his arms. Gary squeaked, but he wrapped his arms around Alexis and squeezed him hard. Alexis could feel the same emotion in Gary as he was feeling, and he suspected they both needed this.

They'd thought they were alone, but they weren't anymore.

"We might be bringing trouble to your village," Tomlin warned.

That was enough to get Alexis to take a step back. "What do you mean?"

Tomlin and Gary looked at each other. Alexis could tell they weren't sure whether to tell Rowan the truth, but the clan needed to know what was happening if they were going to do something about it.

"The Kudlaks are targeting Vila families," Tomlin eventually said. "They know that without us, you can't work against them as hard as you used to. They've been hunting us for several days, and tonight, we were lucky enough to be close by when they finally attacked. Not every family was." He swallowed. "We've heard about so many of them dying at the hands of the Kudlaks. They're organizing and attacking in groups, something we don't know how to deal with. We don't know what to do."

Rowan squeezed his shoulder. "You did the right thing by coming here. We'll protect you."

They would. Now that Alexis had found a place to call home, he wouldn't allow anyone to ruin it, especially not the Kudlaks. He'd been born to fight them, and that was what he'd do.

Boyd might not be a Krsnik, but that didn't mean he didn't know Kudlaks. He'd been fighting them since one had killed his sister, and he knew something of their behavior.

They always hunted alone or in pairs. Even when they had a nest, they left their children behind, and they certainly didn't attack entire families of supernatural creatures who could hurt them. No, Kudlaks usually targeted humans because they were easy prey, but this time had been different, and from what Tomlin was saying, it wasn't the first time it happened.

That was enough to worry Boyd. Why were Kudlaks working together? Was it only because some of them wanted to finish killing the clans they'd been working on for so long? Boyd almost wanted that to be it, but it felt too easy. Not all Kudlaks behaved that way, which meant that the ones who weren't hunting Krsniks for that reason had to have another goal.

What was it?

"I'm glad you were honest with me and that you told me all of that," Rowan said. "We can talk again tomorrow, and you can tell me everything your family has been through. I also want you to feel safe here. We don't have shields up yet because we don't have any Vila with us, but it doesn't mean we're not protected. The council is keeping an eye on us because we work for them. You don't have to worry about what will happen tonight, and as soon as you feel up to it, I'd like to talk to you about putting up some shields."

"I'll do that now," Tomlin said. "I don't think I'll be able to sleep without them."

Rowan looked like he wanted to argue, but he didn't. Boyd suspected he knew this was for the best, even though it would mean that Tomlin was exhausted by the time he was done. Boyd had never seen a Vila shield and didn't know anything about their magic, but it couldn't be easy, especially after being attacked by the Kudlaks.

"I'll stay with Tomlin," Jonas said, startling Boyd.

Boyd hadn't noticed him come closer, but he shouldn't be surprised. Jonas had a way of always being at the center of things. He wanted to know everything that was happening, and he never hesitated to give his opinion.

Rowan nodded. "Thank you, Jonas. Clay and I will walk everyone else to some of our empty houses. Do you want to all share the same house, at least tonight? I don't think any of them has enough beds, but we can work something out."

"Tomlin can stay with us for the night," Jonas quickly said. "Alexis is going to stay with Boyd, anyway."

Boyd arched a brow at Jonas, but Jonas didn't see him because he was making a point of not looking at him and Alexis. Whatever was going on, he was trying to avoid telling them. The fact that his cheeks were flushed didn't help hide it, and Boyd wondered if maybe Jonas liked the sight of Tomlin.

He didn't think Jonas would try to seduce him tonight of all nights. He would never do that after what Tomlin and his family had gone through. That didn't mean he didn't want to spend some time with Tomlin, though.

Boyd had no idea what would come of that or even if anything would, but he was curious. The next few days were going to be interesting.

"If Tomlin is fine with it, it is with me," Rowan said.

"Thank you," Tomlin said as he inclined his head. "I appreciate you welcoming me into your home. I don't think we need to stay in the same house. We have several families with us, and once the shields are in place, we'll all feel safe enough to separate."

"Perfect," Rowan said with a nod. "Why don't you tell me how many families you have so we can choose the houses?"

Gary patted Alexis's shoulder, then stepped away from him and toward Rowan. Alexis looked like he wanted to drag the older man into his arms again, but he let him go. He and Boyd watched as the group followed Rowan down the road, and now that they out of hearing, Boyd allowed himself to ask the question that had been burning his lips.

"You know Gary," he said to Alexis.

Alexis nodded. "He was in my can. I thought everyone was dead, but I was wrong, and it's a lot. I apologize for not introducing you."

"I didn't expect you to do that today of all days. It was clear you were all over the place, and I think you still are."

Alexis nodded, but he was already turning his attention to Jonas. Boyd snickered when he saw that Jonas was staring at Tomlin as if he were a giant ice cream, and he couldn't believe what was in front of his eyes.

"You can take my room," Alexis told Tomlin. "I've only slept there a few nights, because I met Boyd as soon as we arrived."

"He's your mate?" Tomlin asked.

"He is. I haven't fully moved in with him, but you don't have to worry and can stay in my room for as long as you need."

"Congratulations, and thank you." Tomlin looked around, and his gaze stopped on Jonas. "We did the right thing by trying to find this place, and I'm glad we got here. We can finally go back to life as it should be and feel safe."

That was all Boyd had ever wanted and why he'd started hunting Kudlaks. In the beginning, he'd yearned for revenge, but after a few hunts, he'd realized he would never get it. He didn't know the Kudlak who'd killed his sister. He didn't even know if that Kudlak was male or female. He couldn't get revenge if he didn't find out, and the only person who could tell him was that Kudlak.

So Boyd had changed. He'd started hunting Kudlaks to keep everyone safe and not only to avenge his sister. He'd done a good job for many years, but he was tired of it.

What was happening with the Kudlaks wasn't his business anymore. He'd told Rowan he didn't want to be a hunter, and he wasn't. Tonight had been his last hunt, and he'd never have to deal with a Kudlak again.

Except that he might have to. If what everyone was thinking was correct, the Kudlaks would eventually attack the village. That meant Boyd had to be ready to defend himself and the people he cared about. He might not want to hunt or hurt anyone, but if it meant keeping his people safe, he wouldn't hesitate.

Jonas guided Tomlin away, and Boyd peered down at Alexis. He looked better than he had after the attack, but Boyd still felt unsteady about him. He needed to take Alexis home and take care of him, but he wasn't sure Alexis was ready for that. What happened tonight had been unexpected, and it was clear Alexis wasn't sure how to deal with any of it.

"You don't have to wrap your mind around all of this tonight," Boyd said as he hooked an arm around his mate's shoulders. "It was a lot, and you lost too much blood. You need some rest."

He could see Alexis wanted to argue, probably so he could go with Jonas and Tomlin or even with Rowan to help settle the families, but he didn't. Instead, he nodded and leaned against Boyd.

Boyd liked that. He wanted his mate to be able to lean against him, even if it wasn't during a fight. Alexis had to know that whatever he needed, Boyd would always try to give it to him.

"Ready to go home?" he asked.

Alexis glanced around again. The other hunters had scattered, all of them headed to their homes. Caroline was the only one hanging back, but as soon as Alexis waved at her, she rushed away, probably yearning for a shower and a bed like Boyd was.

Alexis looked up at him. "Yeah. I'm ready to go home."

He was calling Boyd's house their home. They might not have moved in together officially, but it wouldn't be long, and Boyd couldn't wait. He wanted them to make the house their home and maybe raise a family there. He wanted those walls to see their future and for them to grow old between them.

This was only the first step to making that happen.

Too many things had happened tonight, and Alexis didn't know where to start. He was worried about what was happening with the Kudlaks and the possibility that they'd target the village. That meant he needed to be healthy and ready to act as soon as he could, but right now, there was no way he'd be able to fight.

Rowan and Clay were good leaders, but Alexis wasn't sure they fully understood what being a clan leader meant. They'd need to keep the village safe, which meant organizing their people. They needed more shields, guards, and patrols. There was so much to do, and Alexis wanted to help, but he wasn't sure where to start. He'd never done anything like this.

"You're thinking too hard," Boyd said as he walked next to Alexis.

They were holding hands, something Alexis had never done before—although, to be fair, he'd never been in a relationship before Boyd. He wondered if Boyd had taken his hand because he wanted to make sure Alexis wouldn't fall on his face. It could happen, even though they were walking down the road. Alexis felt exhausted enough that he wouldn't have a problem falling asleep as soon as his head hit the pillow. Hell, he might even fall asleep if he stopped moving, which was why he kept on walking.

"I can't turn off my brain," he complained.

He wished he could. There was nothing he could do about any of this right now, but knowing it wouldn't stop him from freaking out over it. How was he supposed to not think about the danger they were in? Or about the way the Kudlaks had killed his clan and his family? Or even about what would happen when they continued trying to kill the last members of the clans, like Alexis and Rowan?

Boyd squeezed Alexis's hand. "I know you're worried, and you have every reason to be. I'm worried, too. But there's nothing we can do about any of this tonight. Obsessing over it and not sleeping won't help you. If anything, it'll make the situation even worse, and that's not something we want to happen. The village needs you at your best, and not sleeping after losing so much blood won't be you at your best."

Alexis grunted. "I'm aware of that. It doesn't mean it's easy not to think about what happened tonight."

"I know. I don't expect you not to think about it, especially since you found one of the people you called family alive. I'm glad you have him again."

Alexis didn't want to think about Gary and what had happened to him. Every time he did, his eyes started burning, and he felt he was about to cry.

He could only imagine what Gary had gone through. He wasn't a fighter and never had been. When Kudlaks had attacked their village, Alexis had been out on a hunt. It had to have been terrifying. Gary had probably watched as people he loved were killed, as the place he'd called home was destroyed, and he'd lost everything. Alexis had, too, but he felt he was better equipped to deal with that. He'd always known he'd lose people. He'd always known he'd die in battle.

But now he had one more reason to make sure that never happened. He'd been born to fight Kudlaks and to protect people, including Boyd and Gary. To make sure he could, he'd have to survive every hunt he went on.

Luckily, he had a lot of experience.

He tripped and stumbled. He didn't fear falling on his face because Boyd was there, and sure enough, his mate grabbed him around the waist and pulled him against his chest. Alexis closed his eyes for a moment, told himself to stop obsessing over things he couldn't change, and opened them again.

Only to have Boyd swoop him up into his arms bridal style.

"I can walk," he said.

"I know. You were walking until now."

"Why are you carrying me, then?"

"Why shouldn't I? You were hurt, and you're still weak from the blood loss. My job is to protect you, and that's what I'm doing."

"There isn't any Kudlak around."

"No, but the ground would have hurt you if you'd fallen."

Alexis couldn't help but smile. "So you're protecting me from the ground?"

Boyd grinned at him. "Exactly."

Alexis had been forced to be strong for a long time. Even after finding Caroline and Jonas, he'd always felt he needed to protect them. Caroline would kick his ass if he ever told her that, but it was true. He'd felt like their unofficial leader, which meant he'd needed to be strong. He'd been the one to take care of them, make sure they were okay, and give

Caroline what she needed after the hunts. They'd taken care of him, too, but not like this. He'd never had anyone to care for him so completely. Even with them, he'd never allowed himself to show them how much he hurt and how terrified he was.

But all of that, he could do with Boyd. His mate wouldn't care that he was scared. He wouldn't care that he was anxious about the future. He'd take care of him through all of it, and Alexis could finally stop being strong even when he didn't feel he was.

"Let me take care of you," Boyd murmured.

"You won't have to ask me twice. I'm exhausted."

"Allow yourself to rest. You're not alone facing all of this anymore."

"Because I have you." Even though Alexis hadn't been alone before, this was different.

"You have me, Kendrick, and Chris, and everyone else. You're understandably worried about what the Kudlaks are doing and what it could mean for the village, but you won't have to defend us on your own. Even if there aren't enough people here, the council protects us, too. They won't allow anything to happen to us."

Alexis still wasn't entirely sure about this whole working-for-the-council thing, but he didn't make that kind of decision anymore. That was all Rowan and Clay, and Alexis needed to trust them. If he didn't, he should leave the village.

He had no plans to do that.

He might not understand where Rowan and Clay were coming from, but he did trust them to keep everyone safe. He also couldn't imagine anything worse than being in their place, and he'd happily leave the major decisions to them.

He leaned against Boyd's chest and closed his eyes. Luckily, the house wasn't far. Nothing was in the village. Alexis had poked around and discovered that a wolf pack had lived here before. This place had been their home, and while over the decades, the pack had dwindled then disappeared, this place wouldn't vanish from the map. It had become home to a new group of people, and it felt like a sign. The pack was gone, but the clan was here to stay.

When Boyd started climbing steps, Alexis opened his eyes. They were home, but Boyd still didn't set him down. He struggled with the front door for a moment but finally managed to push it open. Then he carried Alexis straight up the stairs to his bedroom. He made to put Alexis down on the bed, but Alexis shook his head.

"I need to shower before I go to bed."

Boyd didn't look convinced. "You'll be okay in the shower on your own? Do you need me to stay with you?"

"Need, no, but I *want* you to stay with me."

Boyd chuckled. "I don't think you're up for that tonight. How about you shower while I grab something to eat?"

He was right, even though Alexis didn't like it. "Fine. You can get me food."

"I won't be long."

Boyd put Alexis down on the closed toilet, then kissed the top of his head.

Alexis knew he stank of blood, sweat, and death, but Boyd didn't seem to care. Alexis was falling for him so hard and fast that it was dizzying. It was something else he was anxious about, but he told himself he didn't need to be.

However fast and hard he was falling, he was pretty sure Boyd felt the same.

CHAPTER SEVEN

Boyd waved at Pheodora when she walked past him down the street. She blinked at him, then waved back with the hand that wasn't carrying her bag. Boyd had no idea where she'd been, since the stores in the village were still closed, but he supposed it didn't matter.

It was odd to see so many new people in the village. Boyd hadn't talked to all of them yet, and most of the Vila were a bit wary of the hunters. They were used to sharing their villages with Krsniks, and while Alexis had assured Boyd that there had also been humans and other supernatural creatures in the villages, he couldn't help but wonder if they'd been looked at the same way. He didn't mind having people wary of him, though. They'd only arrived at the village a few weeks ago, and everyone was trying to find their footing.

That included Boyd, although he felt he was getting there. After the night Alexis was bitten, Boyd had stopped going on hunts. Alexis had stayed home for a few days, even though he'd complained that he was perfectly fine and could get back to work. Boyd had found out that kissing him was a great way to distract him and keep him at home, so he'd kept that up as long as he could.

He was still terrified at the thought that something could happen to Alexis any time he went out with the hunters. Something *had* happened to him, and he was alive because Boyd had been there.

And now, Boyd wasn't.

Boyd was glad he wasn't going on hunts anymore, but he

was always worried. It was so easy to imagine something happening to Alexis or to one of the other people Boyd cared about. The easiest way to make sure they were safe would be to go with them, but it wasn't something Boyd could do. He'd seen too much blood and had hurt too many people. It didn't matter that they'd deserved it. He couldn't deal with it anymore and was glad that Rowan had accepted that.

It had been easier to settle into this new job than Boyd had expected. After what happened during the last hunt, he'd sat down with Rowan and Clay, and they'd gone over everything needed in the village.

Pretty much everything.

Someone needed to open the grocery store and maybe a few other stores like a coffee shop and a place to get clothes. For now, the village was full of empty businesses, and it felt a bit like a ghost town, even with the new families who had moved in. Boyd couldn't imagine himself working at the coffee shop, but he'd noticed the many yards and green areas were a mess and offered to clean them up and keep them in a good state. It reminded him of his father, and Rowan had jumped on the opportunity when Boyd had told him about it. Boyd was now the official gardener, and while eventually, the job would become easier, for now, there was a lot to do.

It would be easier if Boyd wasn't doing this on his own. He'd been approached by one of the Vila who now lived at the village, who'd asked if he could help, and Boyd had jumped on the opportunity. The opportunity of having someone work with him had reminded him of his father, though, and he couldn't stop thinking about moving his family here.

He hadn't seen them in a long time. They didn't know if he was dead or alive, and they never would unless he contacted them. He desperately wanted to, especially now that he felt he could keep them safe here at the village, but he wanted to talk to Rowan and Clay first. They were the ones who approved any new clan member and anyone who moved into the village, so they'd need to know about it.

Boyd still wasn't entirely sure it was a good idea, mostly because of the pain he'd inflicted on them. Even though they'd be happy to find out he was all right, they'd also be angry and might refuse to come just because of that. He was gearing himself up to contact them because he had to know. It wouldn't be easy after not talking to them for so long, but having Alexis support him helped. Boyd just needed to take that last step, and he would.

Eventually.

"Boyd," a voice said behind him.

He turned to find Tomlin standing there. He got to his feet and rubbed his hands onto his jeans, trying to get them clean. He'd been cleaning out some overgrown bushes, and he was dirty and sweaty.

"Hey," he said.

He had no idea why Tomlin was talking to him. He'd seen the man around the village, but they'd never talked. Tomlin spent a lot of time with his people, helping them settle down, and almost as much time with Jonas. There was something there, but Boyd had kept Alexis from asking Jonas what was going on. When Jonas was ready, he'd tell them.

"Dermot came to talk to me," Tomlin said.

"He told you that he wants to work with me?" He'd already begun working, but Boyd wasn't going to tell Tomlin that if Dermot hadn't.

"He did. Would it be all right with you?"

"Of course. There's plenty of work to do, and I wouldn't say no to some help."

"He'll be happy to hear that."

"Are you their leader?"

Tomlin hesitated. "Not exactly. I took that role while we were on the run because someone needed to, but now that we're here and part of the village, Clay and Rowan are our leaders. It's just hard for some of my people to remember that."

"I can see how it would be. I wouldn't worry too much if I were you. Rowan and Clay don't care about that kind of stuff."

"They're special."

Boyd agreed. Rowan and Clay were giving a new home to many people and along with it, hope. That wasn't something many people could say. "You can tell Dermot to come find me whenever he wants. I'll talk to Rowan so he knows what's happening and that Dermot needs to be paid for this."

"Thank you. I wasn't sure what to think when I found out that humans live here, but all of you have treated us like we belong."

"That's because you do." Much more than the human hunters, in a way.

But Boyd didn't want to think about it like that. It didn't matter that the hunters were human. They did what Krsniks had done for many years, and as far as Boyd was concerned, that was the only thing that mattered.

His phone vibrated in his pocket, and he took it out. He smiled when he saw that Alexis had texted him. When he looked up, Tomlin was staring at him.

"It's Alexis. He's home."

He and Caroline had gone out on Rowan's orders. They'd heard about a Krsnik living in Memphis and wanted to reach out and see if they could convince them to become part of the clan.

"I'll leave you to it, then," Tomlin said with a smile.

Boyd was sorry to cut their conversation short, but he needed to get home. He had plans for Alexis, and he couldn't wait.

He and Alexis had started to fulfill the bond between them,

but it wasn't complete yet. Boyd wasn't bonded to Alexis, but he had plans on changing that as soon as possible. Alexis leaving the village today had put a wrench in Boyd's plans, but he was back, which meant that Boyd could go and do what he'd been planning.

Telling Alexis he was ready for more.

Alexis wouldn't say no. He might try to convince Boyd to think better of it, but Boyd already had. He'd had weeks to feel the incomplete bond and to think about it, and he knew what he was doing.

He had everything he'd thought he'd lost when his sister had been killed. He had a new home and, hopefully soon, his family. Even if he never got them back, he wouldn't be alone because he had his best friends and the clan.

And Alexis.

ABOUT THE AUTHOR

Catherine is the creator of several series, most of them paranormal, including the Whitedell Pride Series and the Gillham Pack Series. While she graduated in translation, she decided to go the writer's way because it was more fun to create her own stories and characters.

She's been living in Italy for more than twenty years, but she's a daughter of the North—Belgium to be precise—and she misses it so much that she's already planning to move back.

She loves pizza—probably too much—her son, her pets, and of course, books. She sneaks some reading time into her schedule every time she has five minutes free from writing, demands from her various pets and son, and lastly, housework.

Connect with her:

lievens.catherine@gmail.com
BookBub: https://www.bookbub.com/authors/catherine-lievens
Website: https://authorcatherinelievens.com/
Facebook: https://www.facebook.com/catherine.lievens.9
Facebook Group: https://www.facebook.com/groups/411788002341528/
Twitter: https://twitter.com/authorCLievens
Newsletter: http://eepurl.com/c-uvKn

www.ingramcontent.com/pod-product-compliance
Lightning Source LLC
Chambersburg PA
CBHW060639130626
46555CB00002B/869